Even Cowbots Get Blue Balls

Queer, Smutty Stories

S. Park

Microcosm Publishing
Portland, Ore

EVEN COWBOTS GET BLUE BALLS
Queer, Smutty Stories

© 2022 S Park
© This edition Microcosm Publishing 2022
First edition - 3,000 copies - December 7, 2022
ISBN 9781648411014
This is Microcosm #676
Cover by Nicholai Avigdor Melamed
Edited by Lydia Rogue

To join the ranks of high-class stores that feature Microcosm titles, talk to your local rep: In the U.S. **COMO** (Atlantic), **FUJII** (Midwest), **BOOK TRAVELERS WEST** (Pacific), **TURNAROUND** (Europe), **UTP/MANDA** (Canada), **NEW SOUTH** (Australia/New Zealand), **GPS** in Asia, Africa, India, South America, and other countries, or **FAIRE** n the gift trade.

For a catalog, write or visit:
Microcosm Publishing
2752 N Williams Ave.
Portland, OR 97227
https://microcosm.pub/Cowbots

Global labor conditions are bad, and our roots in industrial Cleveland in the 70s and 80s made us appreciate the need to treat workers right. Therefore, our books are MADE IN THE USA.

Did you know that you can buy our books directly from us at sliding scale rates? Support a small, independent publisher and pay less than Amazon's price at **www. Microcosm.Pub**

Library of Congress Control Number: 2022014434

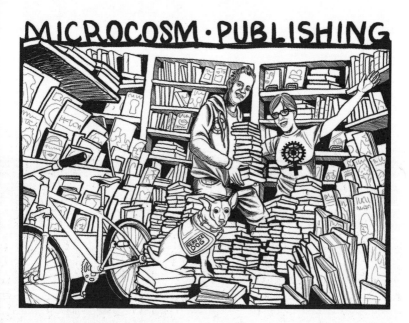

MICROCOSM·PUBLISHING

MICROCOSM PUBLISHING is Portland's most diversified publishing house and distributor with a focus on the colorful, authentic, and empowering. Our books and zines have put your power in your hands since 1996, equipping readers to make positive changes in their lives and in the world around them. Microcosm emphasizes skill-building, showing hidden histories, and fostering creativity through challenging conventional publishing wisdom with books and bookettes about DIY skills, food, bicycling, gender, self-care, and social justice. What was once a distro and record label was started by Joe Biel in his bedroom and has become among the oldest independent publishing houses in Portland, OR. We are a politically moderate, centrist publisher in a world that has inched to the right for the past 80 years.

CONTENTS

Introduction

*F*ICTION IS A LIE.

That's what makes it fiction, after all. If these stories were true, they would be shelved over in the biography section, even given the steamy bits. But they're not true. There's no way any of us are going to meet a lonely nanotech intelligence, a gay vampire out cruising, or a demon taking a break from the pit.

There are bigger lies, though. Lies that are told as if they were truth. Often we're raised on these lies; lies about true love, lies about the evils of sex, lies about how to treat those we become intimate with.

These stories are set in worlds that are very unlike our own, worlds where strange and fantastical things are possible. But I have done my best to use those lies to tell the truth. To say that love is bigger, broader, and wilder than the constraints of a single, heterosexual, destined eternal mate. That sex can be deeply intimate, but that it can also be fun, even wholesome. That life-long commitment and happily ever after are never promised to anyone. And that honesty, communication, negotiation, and consent lead to good—and hot, steamy, sexy, even kinky—things.

This book isn't a how-to manual or a moral primer. I've always said, though, that I put my own experiences into my stories, through the "anything in possible" lens of science fiction and fantasy. And in my experience, consensual erotic encounters are a good time for all. I hope the stories here will be a good time for you too, reader. Go, enjoy!

Hellspawn

*V*ictor always did the violent things, so that other people wouldn't have to.

This wasn't to say that Victor didn't enjoy violence. He very much did. That was *why* he held the position he did. For him, being part of the Army of God was much more literal than for most priests, and he relished every moment of it, most of the time.

Never before, though, had he feared for his life in quite the way he did now.

He ducked aside from the demon's forward lunge, one of his blades deflecting the thing's absurdly huge sword, but despite that weight it was lightning-fast, and it was only the second blade in Victor's other hand that stopped it from gutting him.

The creature snarled, showing fangs, though its face was otherwise that of a handsome young man. Demons could be like that, sometimes. It had curved red-orange horns bracketing a tousle of dark hair, and clawed hands, while its eyes glowed a hellish red, but otherwise looked entirely human. The demon wore ordinary clothing, too; black jeans, a red collared shirt, a black sportscoat, but with bare feet, also clawed. It had seemed to pull the sword from out of nowhere when Victor attacked it.

God above, though, it was *fast*, faster and smarter than any demon he'd ever fought. What rank could this hellspawn be? He'd fought demon lords before, and they were powerful, but they tended to rely on Satanic magic that Victor could counter, and this thing was matching him with pure physicality.

Metal rang against metal in the riverside park, but it was three in the morning, and this city—barely a city, more of an oversized town—wasn't the kind that never slept. So there was no one to see, save the demon hunter and his unexpectedly gifted quarry.

"Will you give up and go away already?" snarled the demon, knocking one of Victor's blades wide with such force that he nearly lost it.

"Never," replied Victor fiercely, using the way the demon's huge sword swung so far to the outside with that blow to bring around his other sword. He didn't manage a significant strike, but he scored a deep line along the creature's bicep.

"Oh, come on!" it growled as wetness suddenly soaked its suit jacket. It spun, and this time it didn't matter how perfectly Victor countered the strike, the force was inhuman, knocking his sword from his hand.

He grinned, though, for it was his right hand. He was ambidextrous, so that was no problem, and his right pocket held a vial of holy water. Even as he somehow managed to dodge another swift strike, and counter yet another with his remaining blade, he pulled the little bottle out and uncorked it with his teeth. Then, with a shout of triumph, he flung it over the demon.

It shouted in pain, falling back, and Victor let his sword's tip drop, panting in relief. He'd gotten the hell-born thing.

Then with a snarl it lunged at him, and it was all he could do to bat the creature's massive blade aside just far enough to score a line across his forearm instead of impaling him. He couldn't stop the rest of its momentum, though, so it crashed into him at waist level, knocking him to the grass, ending up sitting atop him. One clawed hand gripped his throat, and the other yanked Victor's remaining sword out of his hand by the blade, heedless of the cut to its palm. Victor flinched, awaiting death, but the demon just kept him pinned, panting as it sat atop him.

After a moment it groaned. "Fuck, that hurts. Ugh. What the hell is your problem?" It lifted its wounded hand to its lips and licked up a streak of shocking red blood.

Victor gaped up at the thing. "My *problem?* You're a demon! What am I supposed to do, ignore you and let you rampage?"

"Oh for fuck's sake. I have no intention of 'rampaging'. Gods. I was just going to the fucking diner for a late night snack, you lunatic."

Victor took far too long to formulate a response to that, but finally he blurted out, "But you're a demon!"

"Yes, and I'm craving cheese sticks, okay? What kind of maniac carries holy water around, anyway? That hurt like hell!"

"…a demon hunter?" was all Victor could think to say.

"Oh." The demon blinked down at him with its glowing eyes. "Right. Well, uh… Could you *not* hunt me? I swear, I'm just hungry. For fried cheese, not like…souls or babies or whatever."

"You're supposed to be in hell, demon!" It should have been. Its clothes were still wet with holy water, and some of it had definitely splashed across the demon's face, but it didn't seem to have had any effect other than pain. Not even a burn mark! The hellspawn should be dead or at least banished by now. Holy water was powerful. He'd never encountered a demon who could shrug off its effects, not even the Lords of Hell.

"My *name* is Corson," said the demon, suddenly grinning toothily. "And no thanks, Hell is terrible. Ever been there?"

Victor stared at the demon. "…no." Something was nagging at the back of his head suddenly. Corson. Why did he know that name? One generally didn't learn demons' names, they were shy about them. Giving his out meant Corson was being astonishingly reckless, or… Oh *fuck.*

"Corson. As in the Warden of the West, Corson?" Mary, Jesus, and Joseph, no wonder holy water hadn't done much. You couldn't fling a little liquid on one of the four cardinal Princes of Hell and expect it to dissolve him like some minor imp.

"Yup! Not that I have much to ward these days. The Boss decided to reorganize with that circles business, and I didn't get signed up for one. Been bored out of my mind for centuries now."

"Ah…" *Oh God.* Victor had been caught by one of the half dozen most powerful demons in all of Hell. And yet the creature could have killed him at any time in the last few minutes, and hadn't.

"Look, please, if I let you up, will you promise to not try to kill me?"

Victor looked at the demon for a long moment, taking in its— his—earnest expression, then, against his better judgment, said, "Very well. I so swear."

"Oh, we're doing oaths, huh? Sure, I swear to... Uh... I don't know, not rampage, if you leave me alone? Is that good enough?"

"...yes."

"Great!" Corson let go of Victor, rising gracefully and making his sword vanish into nowhere with a sheathing motion. Then he winced. "Ugh. I just about ought to demand you pay for this jacket. I liked this jacket! It was stylish! Now it's got blood all over it."

"Ah, sorry?" Victor was surprised all over again. A demon who cared about fashion.

"Eh, whatever." A shimmer ran over the demon, and though Victor could still see that he was inhuman, he could also tell that to most people Corson would now look perfectly ordinary, not even showing bloodstains, let alone his horns, fangs, or claws.

"Oh. Here, lemme take care of that." Corson was standing right beside Victor suddenly, and Victor jumped when the demon took his hand. He ran a finger across the cut he'd left over Victor's forearm, and to Victor's surprise the cut vanished behind that touch. Corson let go and licked his finger off with relish. "There!"

"Ah... Thank you." Victor shook himself and went to get his lost blade, then donned the duster he'd discarded at the start of the fight and tucked the short swords away inside it. He wore the long coat for just that reason, even though he knew it made him look absurdly melodramatic.

"So, come with me for cheese sticks?" said Corson, beaming at him cheerfully.

Victor, who'd thought he'd already used up his stock of surprise, blinked at Corson. Victor knew it was absurd, but to be honest, he'd been considering hitting up an all-night establishment himself, after doing his usual sweep. "All right," he said.

"Great!"

Which was how Victor Lewis, nominal Catholic priest and enthusiastic demon hunter, ended up at an all-night greasy spoon at 3:30am, sharing an appetizer plate with a Prince of Hell.

"So why demon hunting? I mean, I don't know a lot about mortals, but I gather that's a pretty unusual occupation?" said Corson, around a mouthful of onion rings.

Victor swallowed his own bite and said, "A combination of things, really." He didn't know why he was telling a demon this, but he didn't get a chance to talk about it much. "My family on my father's side, to begin with, are very, very, very Catholic. Irish immigrants and proud of it. When they noticed I was, well…mostly not inclined towards women, let's say, they decided this meant I was for the priesthood." Victor rolled his eyes. "I decided it meant I was for leaving the church, but I didn't manage to get a scholarship, and they had enough money to hold over my head. So I began a religious studies major and promised to go into the seminary after that. I thought it was a lie when I said it."

"But it wasn't?" said Corson, head tilted to the side, crimson, inhuman eyes warm and curious. Victor could catch just enough of his illusion to know they'd be an ordinary brown when most people looked, but he could still see the red. Somehow it no longer bothered him.

"No. I was also taking every single martial arts course the school offered. Violence has always been my love. Always. I'm not a peaceful person. I never have been."

Corson nodded. "Yeah, I understand that."

"Given how well you fight, I'm sure you do." Victor couldn't help but smile. "But one of the religion professors noticed, and gently hinted that there were priestly jobs besides preaching and ministering, that I might be suited for. When I got to know him better and confessed my…inclinations, he said that vows of chastity could be waived for those who risked their lives to protect the flock. And I never thought I could have a career fighting, you know? Joining the military was so impersonal, so regimented. Not for me. But being able to battle for the safety of humanity with my own hands? Oh yes! So I was in, at that point."

"I getcha. So you fight demons all the time?"

"Not just demons. Real Satanists, eldritch cultists, any supernatural threat to the church and to this place. Ah, no offense."

"Nah, none taken. I've fought plenty of demons myself. They don't just let you leave Hell, you know." Corson rolled his eyes. "Which is total nonsense. I have literally no domain anymore. No souls to guard, no sinners to punish. Hell was just sitting around doing nothing all day, every day. I sometimes thought I'd go totally mad from it."

"I can imagine," said Victor, nodding.

"My only relief was when I got to speak with some of the damned. I even talked a few of them into tutoring me!" Corson beamed with boyish enthusiasm. Despite Victor being certain the demon prince had to be far his elder, he suddenly felt old.

"Oh?"

"Yes! All the pagans end up in Hell, you know. But the ones who weren't sinners by their own laws don't get punished, they just sort of hang around. So a ton of history's greatest warriors are down there. I've learned from as many as would teach me!" Corson bounced in place on the booth's seat. "And since most of the old pagans were before gunpowder, I picked up pretty much every ancient weapon. Sword and spear are my two favorites, though, definitely. Guns are so… Ugh. And they're lousy against demons."

Victor grinned, bright and sharp. "I know. That's why I carry swords. And holy water."

"Hah! Yes. Good thing I'm not so easily dismissed by it!"

"Ah… Yes, I guess so."

Corson grinned and reached out, poking Victor in the arm. "Hey, don't sound so uncertain about my being still alive. I'd be pretty damn pissed if I'd been sent back down to Hell to rebuild a corporeal body and start all over. I've done that way too often when the Boss' minions have managed to off me."

"So… What, you've been fighting your way out of Hell repeatedly?"

"Exactly." Corson's grin didn't fade one bit.

"Well, I suppose that explains why you're so good. To be honest, I've never had such a challenge."

"Me either! When I've been killed by the idiot imps of Hell, it's been because they outnumbered me, not because any one of them outfought me. Though a few of the Lords take a little work." Corson rubbed the back of his neck. "Anyway, you're really good! It was almost fun to fight you, except the bits where you wanted to kill me."

"Indeed." Victor couldn't help but grin. It was true. He didn't love his job because of his faith. He knew it was real, or real enough to have an effect on demons, but he didn't care for the saints, for Jesus, for God. He wanted to fight, that was the long and short of it. Fighting Corson had been intense beyond any other fight he'd had.

Victor took the last cheese stick, his smile daring Corson to do something about it. Corson laughed and picked up another onion ring. "You're fun," he said.

Victor eyed Corson. "What does that mean?"

Corson shrugged. "Whatever you want it to mean? I just want to live up here, away from Hell, and have a little fun now and again. If 'fun' means you... What kind of fun do *you* want?"

Victor snorted. "Most of the time my idea of fun is killing demons."

Corson laughed. "Well... I mean, it just sends me back down, so I wouldn't be dead-dead. But I'd rather not do that one right now, if it's all the same to you. Got any other thoughts?"

"My usual list of vices are hard to find at the moment. The bars are closed at this hour, and..." Victor trailed off, his eyes fixing on Corson as the thought he'd had the very first time he'd seen the demon, that he looked handsome, the way demons sometimes could but usually didn't, floated through his mind.

"And?" prompted Corson.

"And I don't have a partner right now, so I can't go home and fuck," said Victor finally.

Corson blinked at him, his cheeks flushing pink. "Oh. Er. Huh." He tilted his head to one side, his expression curious. "You said you liked guys, right?"

Victor lifted both his eyebrows, suspecting where this was headed. "With a few notable exceptions, yes."

Corson grinned again, still flushed, but with all the cocky confidence of youth—or perhaps of royalty—said, "How do you feel about bedding demons?"

Victor couldn't keep from laughing. Not even at Corson, just at the situation itself. "My teachers were quite clear that it's a terrible idea. Succubuses and incubuses are not to be trifled with, etcetera."

"You're not a student now, though," said Corson.

"I assume you enjoy bedding humans?"

"Oh yeah. My girlfriend is human. Although she'd make an *amazing* demon." Corson's expression went dreamy, and Victor shook his head.

"We're probably not all that compatible, though," said Victor, a little astonished he was even considering this.

"Huh? Why not?"

"Because the people I'll bottom to are even rarer than the women I like," he said plainly.

Corson turned absolutely crimson. "Oh. Uhm. Actually, that means we're, uhm, super compatible. I, er, really prefer… Uh…"

"The Prince of Hell likes being pinned down and taken, hmmm?" Victor felt a spark of heat in his gut. It seemed he might actually be doing this, mad as it was.

Corson rubbed the back of his neck. "Ah… You could say that, yeah."

Victor laughed, teeth bared in a wolf's grin. "Well, then, little princeling. Why don't we see what fun we can have. Do you have a place here?"

"Er… No, sorry."

"That's fine. My place is on church grounds, though. Will treading on holy ground be a problem for you?"

Corson frowned. "I don't think so? It's less holy than holy water, right? And that hurt but didn't repel me. Maybe it'll hurt a little? But, well…" He cleared his throat, his cheeks flushed. "We can go see, anyway."

"Very well."

Corson paid their bill, and the pair left the diner and walked into town, threading their way amid sleeping streets, seeing almost no one about in the night as it turned slowly towards morning. They eventually arrived at their destination, a modest church in a lower-class residential neighborhood, surrounded by equally modest houses and apartment complexes. The church had an attached priory, but that wasn't where Victor went. Instead, he went to an apartment building that backed on the church property.

"If you live here," said Corson, gesturing at the little quartet of apartments, "you don't live on holy ground. The church lawn felt uncomfortable, but I don't feel anything here."

"Interesting. It's legally a parcel with the church lot, but I suppose that has nothing to do with which bits got blessed," said Victor. "I guess that simplifies things, though. Come on up." He led the way up the stairs to a second-floor apartment, unlocking and opening the door, then holding it open for Corson, who padded in and looked around curiously.

"Huh. Nice place."

"Thank you." Victor smiled. It *was* a nice place. It was meticulously clean, and though it wasn't cluttered, he'd made a point to decorate it with things he liked. Quality, solid furniture, carefully chosen paintings, a few sculptures tucked here and there on the bookshelves amid the books, none of it on any particular theme, but all of it working well together.

"I thought human men living alone usually had just…I don't know, posters and stuff, and bookshelves made out of cinder blocks, and that kind of thing?"

Victor laughed. "Some men, yes. I'd like to think I have a little bit of taste now and then, though."

"I'm told I have no taste whatsoever." Corson laughed. "But I like your place. Dunno what that says about your taste."

"Who knows? I decorated for myself, not for visitors, though."

"Hah. What's your bedroom like?"

"Straight to the point. Admirable, really." Victor shook his head at Corson's obvious eagerness. "Come, then."

Victor's bedroom was much like his front room, a solid, four-poster bed, more bookshelves, an old-fashioned roll-top desk lined with pigeonholes, and several comfortable chairs. Art adorned the walls here too, and was scattered on the bookshelves, along with a few personal keepsakes. Corson's faintly-glowing eyes took it all in, and he smiled. "Nice. This is the best part, though," he added, plopping down on the bed.

"I see." Victor laughed. "So, my hellspawned friend. We should speak of our desires before attempting them, I think."

"Yeah." Corson nodded. "Prevent any unpleasant surprises."

"And make sure we both enjoy ourselves, yes. What you said... It rather suggested to me that you don't merely bottom, that you *submit*," said Victor, feeling a tight coil in his stomach as he thought of that. To have a Prince of Hell not merely under him, but pliant and willing, answering to his every whim... He licked his lips as he looked at Corson.

The demon's cheeks flushed pink. "Ah. Yes. Yes, uhm, Sir." He ducked his head and looked up at Victor, standing beside the bed, through his lashes.

"Well then, why don't we continue this negotiation with you where you belong? On your knees at my feet."

Corson's eyes went wide, and he instantly slid off the bed to kneel beside it. Victor sat on the bed and smiled as Corson shifted to kneel directly beside his feet, forehead pressed to his leg just below the knee.

"Very good," said Victor. "So. What is off-limits for me to do to you?"

"Er. Not much. I'd rather not die?" Corson glanced up, brow furrowed in thought. "Oh! No calling me 'boy' in any way. No 'good boy,' no 'bad boy,' nothing. You can call me baby or you can call me a fucking whore or anything else you like, just not that."

"Understood."

"Beyond that, I have an inhumanly high pain tolerance, and I have yet to encounter a sex act I was repulsed by, though some interest me more than others. Roughness, pain, blood, the feeling of being helpless and used… Those are the big ones I like. Anything else is fine, though, Sir."

"Hmm. I see. I don't feel in the mood for anything truly extreme tonight, or I might ask some specific questions. Just now, though, fucking you and hurting you sound just fine. Bondage is good?"

"Yes, Sir." Corson nodded. "What about you, is there anything I should be careful not to do?"

"Not really. So long as you don't fight back, I'm quite confident in my ability to manage you."

Corson let out a tiny, choked whine at that. "Y-yes, Sir. I won't, Sir."

"Good." Victor looked down at Corson, and though a small part of him was still incredulous—a Cardinal Demon, here at Victor's feet!—the rest of him was full of eager anticipation. He was at least half-hard already just thinking about it.

So, time to see if this really was going to happen. "Strip," he said in a flat tone of command.

Corson started to get up, and Victor grabbed a handful of his hair and yanked down hard. "No! I didn't say you could rise. Strip right where you are, at my feet, like the miserable damned wretch you are."

"Y-yes, Sir. Forgive me, Sir," stammered Corson, and he immediately shed his bloodied jacket and the marred shirt beneath it, though the skin under that was whole, showing no sign of the injury. With quite a lot of amusing wiggling he got his tightly-fitted jeans off too, revealing tight undershorts, tented up and already showing a damp spot where his cock was leaking pre.

Corson wiggled out of those too, now fully nude, his revealed cock seeming quite ordinary, flushed red and smeared with pearly dampness.

"Adequate," said Victor coldly, looking down at Corson. The demon whined softly in the back of his throat, but returned to his knees, head bowed, awaiting orders. He was breathing fast, Victor could see, and trembling ever so faintly. Delightful.

Victor stood and shed his coat, tossing it aside, chuckling when Corson twitched at the heavy sound the tool-laden thing made when it landed. Next Victor undid his belt buckle, and unzipped his trousers, pulling them down just enough that he could then reach in and pull his cock out. "Here, hellspawn. Suck it."

"Yes, Sir. Thank you, Sir," said Corson, shifting and rising up on his knees so that he could immediately lick along the length of Victor's thick shaft. He swirled his tongue around, deliberately being messy, coating Victor's cock with saliva. Once that swift task was done he took the head of Victor's cock into his mouth and sank down, swallowing the whole of it in one expert motion. Victor felt Corson's nose against his belly, the demon's throat, hot and tight, squeezing around his head, and knew he wasn't going to last terribly long.

Well, there was always round two, later.

For now Victor took a handful of Corson's hair, twisting his fingers until he got a muffled whimper around his cock, and began to use that to guide Corson, pulling the demon back then yanking him down hard. Corson's eyes rolled back, his lashes fluttering, and his hands clutched at Victor's thighs, but he put up no resistance whatsoever, and indeed cooperated, moving in response to Victor's tugs, working his tongue along Victor's cock with each stroke.

"There you go. Good b— Good pet. Good little hellspawn."

Corson moaned around Victor's cock, his fingers digging into Victor's thighs. Victor put his other hand on Corson's head, shifting his grip to grasp the bases of his horns. He pulled hard, forcing Corson's head suddenly down, hearing the helpless, choked sounds the demon let out. They only added to his enjoyment, and the startled little "Mmph!" when he didn't let up, but held Corson on his cock, was even better.

"Getting close, pet. Think you can stay there until I come?"

"Mmmph!" Corson didn't fight at all, he only swallowed, his throat squeezing around Victor's cock, his tongue working at it diligently.

"Very good. My good little demonic whore. Keep doing that." Not that Victor was giving Corson any choice. His grip was iron hard, keeping Corson exactly where he wanted him, Victor rocking his hips just enough to add to his pleasure, feeling it build rapidly.

All at once he was there, tipping over the edge into orgasm, that unique pleasure overwhelming him as Corson continued to work around his cock, the demon swallowing down the seed that shot into his throat willingly, eagerly even.

Victor kept Corson there until he'd spent every last drop, then yanked Corson back and let go.

Corson half-collapsed, bracing his hands on the floor and panting hard, his whole body trembling intensely. "Th-thank you, Sir," he said, breathlessly.

Settling down on the bed, Victor had to catch his own breath, aftershocks of pleasure still running through him. "You are a very good little hellspawned whore. You've sucked quite a lot of cocks, haven't you, pet?"

Corson drew in a gasp at that. "Yes, Sir." He crawled over to Victor and rested his head against Victor's leg. His breath was slowing but his cheeks were still flushed brightly.

Victor chuckled and stroked Corson's hair, fingers toying with his horns idly. He heard a little hitch of breath from the demon at that, and filed that information away for later. "Perhaps you're an incubus, hmm?"

Corson made another little whining sound. "If... If it pleases you to say so, Sir."

"Incubuses are some of the lowest demons, aren't they?"

Corson swallowed and nodded. "Yes, Sir."

"You have come very low now yourself, Prince of Hell. Kneeling to a mere mortal like me, letting me use you. Hardly princely."

Corson only whined again, squirming where he rested against Victor's leg.

"I think you should be lower still. But here, I'm far too dressed. Begin by removing my boots."

"Yes, Sir. Of course, Sir." Corson bent and began unlacing Victor's boots. He pulled each one off carefully and set it aside, then removed Victor's socks too, without being asked. He began to straighten, but Victor gave the back of his head and light cuff. "Now kiss my feet, Prince of Hell."

Corson gasped, then bent swiftly, pressing his lips to Victor's feet, first one, then the other.

"There, that's where you belong, hellspawn. Don't lift your head, stay just like that while I decide what else to do with you."

"Yes, Sir," said Corson, staying bent double by Victor's feet, though he was squirming restlessly, obviously very keyed up. God, his submission was beyond thrilling. The demon who'd come closer than any to killing him, one of the most powerful in the world, bowing willingly to him. He could do anything he wanted to Corson, with almost no restraint. His cock twitched as he started to grow aroused all over again. He played a number of scenarios through his mind, before deciding on a place to start.

"Stay there," said Victor as he stood up. He stripped his clothes off, tossing them aside, noticing that Corson had tilted his head to look up from the corner of his eye. Victor laughed. "Like what you see, incubus?"

Corson shivered. "Y-yes, Sir."

"Good. I'm going to get a few things now. Don't move."

Corson stayed bent double on his knees, hands on the floor, forehead nearly touching it. Victor rummaged in his closet until he found what he was looking for, then turned around and took in the sight of the Prince of Hell bowed down like that. God. If they kept doing such things, would it ever lose its edge? With his curved horns and clawed hands and feet, there was no mistaking Corson for a human being. Yet he was built like the most gorgeous young man Victor could imagine, broad-shouldered and muscular, but with a narrow, almost delicate waist and a trimness that suggested a gymnast's athleticism rather than a weight-lifter's brawn. He looked utterly splendid, prostrate and waiting for Victor, and the priest's cock gave another twitch at the sight.

He set down the objects of his search on his nightstand. Steel clinked on steel as the heavy cuffs landed there, but the rope and the bottle of lube were silent. Victor grinned and fingered one more thing, the rosary he still wore around his neck. A lesser demon wouldn't have been able to so much as touch him with it on, of course, but he wasn't sure Corson had even noticed he was wearing it.

Victor rather hoped Corson hadn't. It would be more fun if it were a surprise.

"Up on the bed now, my pet," said Victor, and Corson immediately straightened, but climbed into the bed without actually standing. He was admirably eager to abase himself, it seemed.

"Lie on your back," ordered Victor, and again Corson instantly obeyed. Victor grabbed one of the cuffs from the nightstand then took one of Corson's wrists. The cuffs were heavy leather, lined in fur, with a second reinforcing strap, a sturdy buckle, and an O-ring to allow them to attach to things. He fastened the first snugly onto Corson's wrist, tightening it as much as he could, knowing the padding would keep it from digging in. Corson sighed, his eyes fluttering closed, his body going relaxed, almost limp. Victor noted that too, smiling at the demon's reaction.

The matching cuff took only a moment to put on, and then Victor looped the length of rope through the two steel rings, attaching the cuffs to each other and, a moment later, to the headboard of the bed, that had been built with such things in mind and had a useful slat just at the right place.

"There. Not exactly what I usually mean by 'demon binding' but I believe it will do. Is that secure, my pet?"

Corson tugged at the hands now fastened above his head, wiggling and struggling until he started to pant, but not managing to budge rope or cuffs by a single millimeter. "Y-yes, Sir," he said breathlessly.

"Good." Victor ran his hand down Corson's bare chest, smiling as the demon went utterly still save for the motion of his breathing. "I'm tempted to tie your feet down too, but like this I can quite easily flip you over." Victor grinned as Corson drew in a sharp breath and shuddered.

"Before I do that, though, my captive little hellspawn, I think I'm going to hurt you. What do you say to that?"

Corson gave another shudder. "If— If you want to, Sir. I, gods, do anything you want to me, Sir."

"Needy, twisted little whore. You like pain, hmm? Let's see if you still do when I'm done with you." Victor swung a leg over Corson, sitting on his thighs to pin them down, and smiling at the sight of the demon's hard, flushed cock standing up. He didn't touch it, though. Instead he reached up and pulled the rosary from around his neck. Corson, beneath him, gasped, eyes flying wide open in shock.

Before Corson could react in any other way, Victor pressed the crucifix in the center of his chest. Corson arched under him, pulling hard at the cuffs that held him, and letting out a shocked cry of pain.

Victor lifted the crucifix and regarded the spot where it had touched. It looked reddened, like a sunburn. He stroked a finger over it, and Corson flinched. "Delightful," murmured Victor. Corson was so responsive. He hid nothing, his every emotion showed clearly. It was exactly what Victor liked in a partner.

Next Victor simply let the rosary fall over Corson's chest, the crucifix resting near where it had touched before, the beaded string trailing over his body.

"Ah, fuck!" gasped Corson, arching again, squirming until his wriggling struggles managed to tip the holy object off of him.

Victor retrieved it and regarded the pattern of faint red marks with a smile. Oh, this was going to be *fun*.

He started dragging it over Corson's skin, sometimes slowly, sometimes swiftly. He found the crucifix itself left a deeper, more painful burn, and if he held it in one spot long enough, blisters would form. The beads were obviously less potent, but still painful, and pressing a handful of them against Corson would leave clusters of pink or red dots. Corson cried out and swore and struggled with each painful touch. Victor didn't remotely relent, though he would pause briefly now and then to trace his fingers over the marks he was leaving.

Eventually, when Corson's chest and belly were nearly covered in marks, Victor dipped that touch lower, fingers caressing across Corson's hips and then inward, stopping just short of the demon's leaking cock.

Corson, whimpering with lingering pain, chest heaving, let out a trembling, needy moan. "P-please…"

"Please what?" growled Victor.

"Please, touch me, Sir," said Corson, his tone desperate.

Victor smiled, an evil, sadistic smile, and said, "Needy whore of an incubus. But very well, if you insist." Then he looped the rosary's beaded string around the base of Corson's cock and pulled it tight.

The cry Corson let out was a full-voiced scream, enough to make Victor glad that these were modern, sound-proofed apartments. Victor didn't relent, though, he slid the blessed loop up the length of Corson's cock. The burned streaks each bead left behind weren't visible against the red flush of it, but to Victor's delight, it didn't grow the least bit softer as Corson screamed and writhed and bucked.

When Victor finally removed the beads Corson went completely limp, panting desperately, his entire body trembling. "Oh, f-fuck," gasped Corson.

"Too much?" murmured Victor, still smiling.

"Hell, no!" was Corson's immediate response. "It's…a lot, is all."

"You really are a twisted little hellspawn." Victor laughed and pressed the crucifix against the base of Corson's cock, getting a startled cry, and then held it there until Corson was writhing and screaming again.

"Ah, gods, Victor!" cried Corson, pulling so hard against his restraints the sturdy bed frame began creaking alarmingly, but Victor still didn't relent.

When he finally lifted the crucifix it left blisters and charred hair behind it, a faint wisp of smoke rising, bringing the acrid scent of burned hair with it. Corson whimpered, trembling intensely, eyes rolled back and, Victor noticed, claws dug into his palms hard enough to draw blood. He also noticed that the first few marks he'd left had vanished, healed already. Not surprising, really. A bit disappointing, perhaps, but on the other hand, it meant he could do more, push Corson further, if he wanted.

"You scream beautifully, hellspawn." Victor traced his fingers over the latest burn, savoring the conflicted whimper the demon let out as Victor's hand also brushed his cock. Then Victor rocked his own hips forward, letting his renewed erection rub against Corson's. Victor hadn't needed to touch himself, just the sound and sight of the demon prince suffering had been enough.

Corson moaned weakly, obviously too caught up in pain to fall fully into pleasure. God, this was so good. Victor decided he couldn't wait any longer to seek his own pleasure. He climbed off of Corson, who cracked his eyes open, looking at Victor but not moving to struggle or kick. With a low, pleased chuckle at how completely Corson had succumbed to him, Victor flipped the demon over onto his stomach.

This wrung another intense cry of pain, just short of a scream this time, from Corson, as his burns made contact with the bedding. Corson made no move to fight, though, he only lay still save for his trembling as Victor reached for the bottle of lube.

Victor got his fingers well-slicked with it, then pushed them between Corson's cheeks, finding his entrance, and savoring the breathless, eager moan the demon let out as Victor circled his fingers there. "You want me, don't you, hellspawn?"

"Y-yes," said Corson.

"Just like the incubus you are. Just like a whore. Are you, Prince? Are you my whore?"

Corson whimpered, squirming, and whimpered more sharply as the motion no doubt woke pain in the burns all over him.

"Well? Are you my whore?"

There was another whimper, but Corson said, "Yes…"

"Yes *what*, whore?" said Victor sharply, halting the circling motion of his fingers.

"Ah… Y-yes, Sir! Please, Sir!"

"Good little whore of a demon," said Victor, and pushed one finger into Corson, who moaned shamelessly as it entered him. "There you go."

"Oh… Thank you, Sir," groaned Corson.

Victor pushed his finger in slowly but steadily, rocking and twisting it as he did, beginning to spread Corson open.

Corson whined, then said, "Please, Sir… Please, more?"

"*Definitely* a whore. So eager to be filled," said Victor, but without any bite to it at all, completely enjoying himself. He willingly pushed a second finger in, plunging them both deep this time, then swiftly scissoring them, savoring the gasps and moans that Corson let out as he did.

"How is that, hmm? Do you want more still, my demonic whore?"

"Yes... Gods, *please*, Sir."

Victor finally moved to straddle Corson, pinning the demon's legs between his, lining his cock up, the head pushing against Corson's slicked entrance. Victor was quite well endowed, and had a feeling he'd probably hurt Corson, with how little preparation he'd had. He also had a feeling Corson would like that. So he started pushing in, and smiled when Corson gasped, "Gods, yes, you feel so good, Sir!"

Moving slowly but without hesitation, Victor sank in to the hilt, savoring Corson's whimpers and babbled pleas nearly as much as he savored the demon's tight heat around his cock. He pulled back slowly, teasingly, pausing with just the head of his cock still inside, waiting until Corson let out a whine of frustrated need and then plunging in with one single, swift stroke. Corson arched under him, his cry an outright scream of both pleasure and pain. It was wonderful, heady stuff, and Victor thrust in hard again, then again, making each stroke as strong and deep as he could.

Corson moaned with each thrust, wonderfully responsive, spurring Victor on to take him all the faster, all the harder. God, when had he ever had a lover like this? Corson was so perfect, writhing beneath him, completely submissive to him, taking everything Victor had to give.

"Please, Sir," moaned Corson as Victor continued to take him roughly. "Please, oh please, I need you."

"Need my cum in you, whore? I bet you do. You'd do anything for it, wouldn't you?" "Gods, yes! Anything you want!" Corson clenched tightly around Victor's cock, prompting a low groan of pleasure from him.

"Mmm... So eager for me. I'll give you what you need, then, incubus. Ah..." Victor was panting hard now, thrusting fast, feeling his orgasm building rapidly. He grabbed one of Corson's horns, yanking the demon's head back, using that as leverage to help pound into him all the harder.

"Ah! Oh yes, oh Victor... Oh, please," gasped Corson, still clenching hard, his muscles standing out as he tensed his whole body.

"Ha... Ah... Yes... Fuck yes, you're mine now, demon. *Mine!*" snarled Victor, and he came hard, seeing stars as his orgasm ripped through him, hot seed spurting out into Corson, who let out a cry of utter bliss. Victor felt Corson shudder and spasm beneath him and realized the demon had come untouched, just from the sensation of being taken. *God*, that was amazing.

Victor let go of Corson's horn and rested atop the demon as the last of his orgasm faded, catching his breath, and enjoying the demon's warmth under him. Corson dropped his head face down on the blankets and let out a long, happy sigh, lying completely limp. At length he said, "You fuck like... Like a fucking god. Mmm. That was the best."

"My, I'm flattered. I quite enjoyed myself as well." Victor rolled off of Corson and rose, stretching. "Here, let's get you loose," he added, reaching for the cuffs. Once released, Corson sat up and rubbed his wrists, then tentatively drew his fingers over his chest, wincing.

"Damn. Good thing I heal fast. Not that I'm complaining, really. I'm just sore as hell."

Victor chuckled. "You certainly weren't complaining at the time. Now, though, I think we need a shower. And do you need any of those burns dressed?"

"Nah, they'll be fine soon. But a shower sounds great, I'm a mess." He looked down, and grinned. "The best kind of mess."

As they washed up together, Corson wincing now and then, he said, "So, Victor... I hope it's not too much to ask if this can be something we do again sometime? Maybe even, ah, regularly?"

Victor, perfectly aware that this entire situation was completely mad—a demon hunter and a Prince of Hell as lovers!—still couldn't help but grin and reply, "I can't think of anything I'd like better."

The Alpha Omega

"*H*ere's your desk. We spend some time working remotely, of course, but when you're here on site this is where you'll be."

Carlton's coworker, whose name he'd already embarrassingly forgotten, gestured around the room, half full of people sitting at similar desks. It was partially open plan, with half-walls that you could easily look over, but that provided a hint of privacy.

"You're the only official alpha here," said the coworker giving him the tour. "Everyone else I know is a beta. Although there is... Ah, there he is now. Tony! This is Carlton Savage, the new network specialist." The young man waved at another youthful-looking man who'd just stepped into the room. He was on the short side, with a slender build, but the tight-fitted polo he wore made it clear that he was no couch potato; he was lean, but every muscle was defined by the clinging fabric. "Carlton, meet Tony, who stubbornly refuses to confirm if he's an Alpha or not."

Tony rolled his eyes. "There are anti-discrimination laws for a reason. Nobody's required to disclose. It's not written anywhere on anyone's application forms, and what I like to do in bed has nothing whatsoever to do with how well I manage a computer."

"Come on, Tony. People just like certainty and dislike uncertainty. You used to do sales, you know that." The young man was smiling, and Tony was too, but there was an edge to Tony's smile.

"You just want to know where to put me in the office pecking order. I keep telling you, alpha, beta, or omega, I'm the best one here, I belong on top." Tony's smile widened into a grin, and the other man laughed, but Carlton was sure he saw a hard, even angry glint in Tony's eyes.

"Well, I'm afraid you'll have to share the top now, since Carlton here is an alpha. Boss told me so when he was hired. Right, Carlton?" The young tech's eyes flicked between the two men, a certain anticipation lighting in his eyes, and Carton just barely managed to contain an eye-roll of his own. A beta, looking forward to seeing a dramatic clash between alphas. It was just like being back in high school.

"I'm just here to do a job. There's no reason anybody has to be 'on top' of anybody else," said Carlton. Hopefully he managed to keep annoyance out of his voice. Being an alpha was largely socially beneficial, that was why he'd let it "slip" during his interview. Hiring decisions weren't supposed to favor alphas, but they sometimes did, and he'd badly needed the job. He'd reached the point of applying for fast food and retail work, and a chance to put his actual skills to work at a decent wage had been too good to not play the subtle little social game.

But being an alpha had its down sides. Alphas were rare. To some betas they were spectacles, things to be gawked at. Most people simply didn't seem to understand what Carlton was very sure of by this point. That outside of the bedroom it made little if any difference what your "rank" was, people were people. He'd met alphas who were incompetent idiots, alphas who were the best of the best, and alphas who were bugnuts crazy off in any number of directions, just like he had betas and omegas. People were people.

The ranks pervaded everything, though, despite legislation that said otherwise, and Carlton wasn't going to turn down the chance at desperately needed employment just because he found the way alphas were lionized annoying.

Some of the hard edge in Tony's eyes faded at Carlton's response. His too-aggressive grin turned to a lop-sided smile, something more genuine, and he said, "I'm on top of the response-time stats and the after-hours skee-ball score, that's all. I'm not worried about you pushing me out of either of those. Though if we did after-hours King of the Hill, maybe you'd win. You've got a few inches on me."

Carlton, who had played football in high school and had more like a foot on him, chuckled. "Maybe, though I've learned to never underestimate a short guy." He held out his hand, and Tony took it, his grip firm but not a knuckle-crusher.

"Hah. Yeah." Tony was looking at Carlton with a different sort of light in his eyes, suddenly. Not anger, but interest. "Thanks, by the way. I'm glad I'm not the only one who thinks rank doesn't belong at the office."

"Rank is for the bedroom," said Carlton, and the sigh of disappointment from his coworker made Carton finally let loose the eye-roll he'd been holding back as he let go of Tony's hand. "Don't think I'll be finding you in my bed."

Tony laughed at that. "No, I suppose that's pretty unlikely."

"Yeah. Now, I haven't seen the server room yet, I assume it's near here?" said Carlton, and his coworker of the forgotten name shook off his disappointment and guided him into the next room. He resisted the urge to glance back at Tony. The man had made quite an impression in a very brief span, and Carlton was sure he wasn't going to forget Tony's name any time soon.

•   •   •

Carlton centered his eye on his goal, hand cradling the ball. He drew his arm back, then flipped it forward with all the precision of a life-long dedication to sport. The ball rolled up the ramp, missed the scoring holes entirely, and dropped into the bottom of the skee-ball machine. The score flashed, showing a sadly small number. He'd missed more often than he'd scored, this round.

"Dammit!"

"Here, let me show you how it's done." Tony tossed his ball almost casually, beer still held in one hand, and barely seeming to look at the series of circles, but it arced perfectly up and went through the 100 point hole in the upper corner of the machine, the hardest one to hit.

"How the hell do you do that?" said Carlton.

Tony laughed and took a swig of his beer. "Too much time spent in arcades as a kid. While you were out getting hit in the head on the football field, I was at the mall, getting the high score on skee-ball and DDR."

Carlton chuckled and took a pull from his own beer. They were at an unofficial office happy hour that happened now and then at the boss's favorite barcade. About half the bar's occupants tonight were employees, and things were getting loud as the Friday night relaxation proceeded, helped along by copious amounts of alcohol. Carlton himself was on his fourth beer, and though he could hold his booze, he was feeling nicely relaxed. Tony was on number two, but then he probably weighed about half what Carlton did.

"Victory!" Tony pumped his fist as his own final score flashed. It wasn't quite as high as the very highest score chalked on the scoreboard next to the skee-ball machine, but it was still much better than Carlton's sad attempt.

"Here, see if you can show me what an alpha can do with some balls." Tony laughed and put in another set of quarters, dropping another round of balls into the dispenser.

Carlton gave Tony a flat look. "I thought we weren't doing that nonsense." He and Tony had been coworkers for more than a month now. The topic of rank hadn't come up directly again, but the rest of their coworkers certainly weren't shy about making alpha jokes at both of them. Though Carlton had also seen Tony be the butt of several omega jokes, all based around his height. As if betas—or alphas!—couldn't be short. Sure alphas tended to be taller, and omegas tended to be shorter, but those were only tendencies, not absolutes. Which Tony should damn well know, given how much he got teased about it.

Tony's cheeks turned red. "Sorry. I should know better. It's just so damn all-pervasive."

"Yeah, I know. It's fine, really. I shouldn't complain. Being treated like I'm better than everyone else is only annoying in concept, mostly in practice it's nice enough. Some of the ways omegas get treated is damn shameful."

"I know," said Tony, his voice subdued. "Sorry again. I should probably lay off the beer the rest of the night."

"Eh, it's fine. Now why don't you see if you can give me some tips about what to do with these balls?"

Tony snapped instantly from gloom to cheer. "Ball handling, hmm?" He wiggled his eyebrows suggestively at Carlton. "Sure, I can totally teach you what to do with your balls."

"Ha, ha," said Carlton flatly, but he was smiling too.

They played out several more games, and Carlton managed to get one halfway decent score, though he suspected that was luck as much as anything else. Tony got close to perfect scores every single time. Eventually, though, he said, "Think I might dare one more beer. Want me to get anything for you while I'm at the bar?"

"I want to sit down for a bit, why don't we just pull up a couple of stools?"

"Sure, sounds fine."

They found two open stools at the bar, and Tony ordered a third beer, while Carlton ventured a fifth.

"The whole rank thing is just ridiculous," groused Tony, taking his first swig.

Carlton chuckled. Apparently Tony had some more bitching to get out of his system. "It can be, yes."

"I mean, it's a bedroom thing! And yet everybody feels totally free to comment on it. Me included, in my worse moments. I shouldn't. I know I shouldn't. I have no business thinking about what anybody's junk is like, you know? None. Whatsoever. I guess at least I don't say anything about Sharon. Or about her boyfriend!" He gestured across the room, to where a tall woman was sitting at a table, sharing a big basket of loaded fries with a shorter man, and Carlton winced. He'd heard some of the things other people in the office said. Mostly they weren't to her face, but they were still pretty bad.

The teasing Tony got was annoying enough, but people could be downright crude sometimes about alpha women. Sharon worked in graphic design, and Carlton worked tech support, but he'd worked with her often enough to know she was a perfectly normal woman. Her boyfriend worked somewhere else entirely, so tonight was probably a date night for them. And yes, she was a head taller than him, and yes he was *probably* an omega, but Tony was right, it wasn't anybody's business what their sex lives were like.

"And then there's all the idiotic ideas people have about alpha-omega romance. Like, this idea that as soon as you smell somebody, that it's love. It's just hormones, dammit. That's not love." Tony waved his beer in the air. "I mean really, would you only be interested in somebody if they smelled good? Hmm? Really? Falling in love is a *scent?*"

Carlton chuckled, though he could also feel himself blushing. "Honestly, I've never, er… I mean, I've mostly dated beta girls, you know. It hasn't, er, come up much. I knew an omega girl in college for a little bit, but she was on the pill, so I never smelled anything, and she was obviously not into me anyway."

Tony snorted. "We're humans not animals. And feel for the plight of omegas, my friend. Alphas smell like alphas *all the time.*"

"Yeah, I know. Beth said it was really annoying. She wouldn't let me join her study group, said it'd be too distracting, even without her being in heat. Like, she said something like you did, that she wasn't just a, er...bitch sniffing after a dog, but that it was still distracting when she was worried about a big test, you know?"

"It is. It is so fucking distracting." Then Tony blinked at him and said, "Dammit. I didn't mean to say that, forget I did."

Carlton stared at him for a moment. Did that mean that Tony actually was an omega? "Er. Sure thing. You never said anything."

Tony gave Carlton a long look then, mercurial as ever, grinned and leaned over, inhaling in Carlton's general vicinity. "Thanks. You do smell *damn* good, though. I gotta say."

"Uh... Thanks?"

Tony just laughed and took another pull from his beer. "Don't mention it, and I won't either."

•   •   •

Neither of them did, but Carlton couldn't stop being weirdly aware that Tony might in fact be an omega. He did his best to keep it from changing things, but several times, over the coming months, he could swear he could catch the faintest possible whiff of enticing scent around Tony's cubicle.

He did his best to ignore it.

He didn't always succeed.

It had been a series of very long days. They'd been rolling out an upgrade, which meant the best time to do it was after hours, when people weren't at their desks. But it meant that the IT staff had been doing their regular tech support during business hours and upgrading computers after hours all week, and Carlton was about ready to fall over and die.

The overtime pay would be nice, when all was said and done, so he wasn't complaining *too* much, but it was only Wednesday and he was ready for the week to be over.

"Tony, did you get Robert's... Uh..." Carlton trailed off as the scent that he'd inhaled when taking a breath to speak hit the back of his brainstem. It was just a whiff, but he suddenly knew exactly what Beth had meant, back in college, about how ridiculously distracting pheromone scents could be. To a beta or another omega there would be no scent at all, but to him it was clear as day.

"Hmm?" Tony looked up from his computer.

"Sorry, little brain skip there. Have you done Robert's install yet? He was on my case yesterday, so if you haven't done it already, uhm..." Carlton shook his head, trying to get his libido to shut up. It didn't matter what the cubicle smelled like, it would hardly be appropriate to jump on Tony and do...anything, really, right now. Even if they probably were the only two left in the building. No, that was a terrible thought. He couldn't think that thought. What was he thinking? Right, Robert's update. "Uhm. If you haven't done it already, I should do it before I go home."

"Ah. Yeah, I finished it. I was just wrapping up my reports and I'll be out the door." He paused, glancing around, and added, "You seem a bit out of it, you okay?"

Carlton gave Tony a look. "If I am, I think it's your fault. Did you..." He halted. He'd been about to ask if Tony had forgotten a pill or something, but that was really inappropriate to say at work.

Tony laughed. "Nobody else is here, Carlton. You can say whatever."

"I thought you wanted to keep bedroom things out of work?" he said sharply. He was aware that his pants were getting uncomfortably tight. God above, the more he breathed in, the worse it got.

"Sorry. You're fun to twit sometimes. So serious." Tony grinned, but it was an apologetic sort of grin. "Anyway, I was having some side effects, so my doctor adjusted my dose down. Obviously I think we need to just try a different med, because it looks like it's not quite working."

"You could say that." Carlton shifted. "Damn. I feel like I'm fourteen all over again, here."

Tony snickered. "Glad I could inspire your youthful enthusiasm."

Carlton gave Tony another look and rolled his eyes. "Yeah. Thanks."

Tony outright laughed. "Hey, I'm sorry. I didn't do it on purpose! But I'm sure you survived when you were fourteen, you'll make it now. And I'm about to leave, so I won't be bothering you any further in about ten minutes."

"So helpful. It's going to reek like omega for the next week, probably."

"Oh, probably. Another two days, at least." He grinned.

Carlton groaned. "God. Remind me to only text you if I need anything, then."

"Hey, I have to get this wrapped up here." Tony's smile turned more serious. "Sorry, honestly. But I can't help it. I'll be sure to speak to my doctor so this isn't repeated next month, but seriously, you're a big boy, you'll be fine."

"Hah. Yeah, I guess so." Carlton headed back to his own cubicle, still uncomfortably aware of the tightness of his pants. It really was like being a teenager again. Awkward boners had been par for the course back then. He'd thought he was past that, but then he'd never spent much time around any omegas, that he knew of.

Remembering his high school years, Carlton suddenly turned aside, to the restrooms. He chose the single-occupancy room and locked the door behind him.

God. It really was like being a teenager again. Back then it had mostly been some glimpse of a girl, bending over and showing unintended cleavage or happening to wear a just slightly see-through skirt and walk through a sunny spot, things like that. He hadn't ever approached any of the girls, he'd just tried to think unsexy things, and when that didn't work he'd slunk off to the restrooms to beat out a quick one.

Now, of course, it was the memory of Tony's scent. Though the sight of him was okay, too. Picturing Tony's fit little body in any number of improbable situations was far too easy, especially with the confirmation that he was indeed an omega.

Carlton unzipped and freed his straining cock.

With Tony's scent still lingering in his nostrils, he pictured Tony beneath him. What would it be like to pin the shorter man under him? How would it feel? He'd never been with an omega, so he'd never managed to knot. Porn held knotting up as the be-all of amazing sex. Would it actually be that much better? God, he wanted to find out so badly. His hand stroked up and down his cock, moving faster and faster. Even with the omega scent making mush of his brain, he still couldn't get his knot to swell at all, the base of his cock remained unchanged, but it took only a few minutes before there was a sad spatter of semen in the toilet.

Desire turned instantly to shame. Fuck. It really was just like being fourteen again. He hoped that Tony could keep his promise and get his dose adjusted, or Carlton might have to find a new job.

•　　　•　　　•

Carlton parked his car in the massive driveway, next to at least a dozen others, and headed up to the annual company barbecue.

The boss held it every year at his house, Carlton was told, and everyone looked forward to it. The house was a sprawling, state of the art bungalow, with a massive yard containing a pool and everything else a person could possibly want for throwing a summer party.

"Hey, Carlton! Glad you could make it!" Walter, the boss, greeted Carlton at the door with a shoulder slap. Walter was another alpha, though he'd been happily mated to his omega wife for years, and a proper bonding like that was said to completely change the pheromone responses. He'd have no embarrassing flashbacks to being fourteen.

Carlton pushed the months' old embarrassment out of his mind and shook Walter's hand. "Glad to be here."

"Come on in. Pool's open, there's plenty of beer, and the grilling will start in about an hour."

"Thanks." The house was already crowded, it looked like Carlton was one of the last to arrive. The company wasn't huge, even with people bringing spouses and partners the whole thing would be less than a hundred people.

Carlton liked these sorts of occasions. He wasn't the kind to make himself the center of attention at them, but it was nice to casually mingle and chat, to get in some socializing without needing to go out of his way. He could just hold a drink in hand and wander around, and talk to whoever he ran into.

After an hour or so of wandering, he ran into Robert, one of the sales guys and something close to a friend, when he went to check on the state of the food. Robert was manning one of the big grills, while Walter, of course, handled the other.

Beer in hand, Carlton watched Robert flipping burgers. "One of those for me? I like them medium-rare."

"Sure thing. Oh, hey, think you could do me a favor?"

"That depends." Carlton grinned.

Robert chuckled. "Nothing too awful, I just want to baste some of these, and this bottle is just about empty." He nudged the jug of BBQ sauce sitting beside the grill. "There's another bottle of it in the back pantry. Right off the kitchen. Same label as this one, should be on one of the left-hand shelves. Think you could bring it out?"

"Can do."

Carlton parked his beer beside the grill, then made his way back into the house. The kitchen was easy to find, and the pantry from there. When he stepped inside, though, he found Tony there, pulling a six-pack of spiked soda off the shelf. "Oh hey, Carlton. Nice to see you."

"You too. I'm just getting some... Uhm..." Carlton halted, his brain coming to a screeching halt. He'd thought Carlton had smelled good that night a month ago, but oh god it was ten times stronger now. "Uhm... I was... Uh, what was I doing?"

Tony looked at Carlton in confusion, then his eyes went wide and he said, "Oh fuck. I'm so sorry. Last night..."

Carlton blinked and took a step towards Tony. His body appeared to be moving without him. What was Tony saying? "Huh?"

"I got a new phone. I didn't move my alarms over. I completely skipped a pill and I didn't even realize it. I would be in mid-heat today. I'm probably at least half way there right now. Fuck. No wonder I've been feeling weird today. Damn."

"Oh. That's what…" Carlton licked his lips and took another step. The pantry wasn't large, and there wasn't anywhere for Tony to go. The whole space smelled of omega-musk.

"Uh, Carlton? I really am sorry, but you… Er…" Tony was backed up against the shelves, his expression uncertain. Carlton knew he should care about that, but it was very hard to.

Carlton's heart was pounding, the scent of Tony filling his mind. It was so good, so very, very good. He crowded closer, pushing Tony up against the shelves. His hands grabbed the front of Tony's shirt, holding him there.

"Hey! Earth to Carlton! Stop it!"

Carlton blinked, then he yelped and stepped back, letting go of Tony. "S-sorry!"

Tony shook himself. "I suppose that was about half my fault. But get a hold of yourself, man."

"R-right." Carlton shook his head, trying to shake the scent out of it. God, he couldn't *think*. What was he supposed to do now? Why had he even come in here?"

Tony tilted his head to the side. Suddenly his mercurial grin was back. He stepped up close to Carlton, ducked his head every so slightly, and rubbed his cheek all along Carlton's shirtfront. Then he brushed past him, six-pack still in hand, and paused at the doorway to say, "That's for pinning me to the wall. Have fun!"

Carlton turned and blinked at Tony for a moment, then realization dawned. "You absolute bastard! You scent-marked me!"

"You're not an animal, remember? You'll survive." He gave a cheery wave and vanished back into the kitchen with his prize.

Carlton gritted his teeth, tempted to shout after Tony. Goddamn, the little bastard! Omega-scent was all over Carlton's shirt, he could smell it with every breath. He already had an uncomfortable boner, and ducking into a bathroom would only provide temporary relief unless he managed to somehow wash his shirt.

He rubbed his forehead, trying to gather his wits. God, it was hard to think. What was he even doing in here?

Oh, right, barbecue sauce. He looked around and found the jug. His brain was addled, but not so much that he couldn't do that much. He clutched the jug like a talisman, trying to think about nothing else but getting it back to Robert.

"Thanks man," said Robert, taking the jug. Carlton, now bereft of his talisman, looked around for something else to do to keep his mind from being completely overwhelmed. Sweet god above, all he could smell was Tony's scent. It was completely maddening. He wanted to find the little bastard and pin him down and show him the consequences of his actions.

No, no, he could never do something like that. He had to do *something*, though. Maybe he should just leave the party. He looked around again. He caught a glimpse of Tony, sitting on a bench near the pool, drinking a spiked soda and talking to one of the other IT people.

Carlton stared at Tony and took a step in his direction. Then blinked. Goddammit, no. Anyway, if he just walked straight to Tony, he'd go into the pool.

The pool.

Carlton laughed suddenly. He grabbed his beer from where he'd set it next to the grill and slammed back the other half of the can. Then he strode forward. A little table with an umbrella was perfect, he set the empty can, his watch, and his phone there. He toed off his shoes.

"Carlton?" asked Sharon, who'd been sitting by the table, looking at him curiously.

Carlton gave her what was probably a slightly mad grin and said, "Hey, nobody's using the pool!" Then he took two more long strides and jumped right in.

•　　　•　　　•

"Hey, Carlton?"

Carlton was nearly to his car when he heard Tony's voice and turned around. The shorter man was standing on the asphalt, looking less confident than usual. "I wanted to say I'm really sorry about last week."

"It's fine. Everybody just assumed I was a little too drunk." Carlton smiled. "Anyhow, I probably did deserve it for pinning you to the wall like that, that was really out of line."

Tony shrugged. "I forget what it's like for alphas, sometimes. I have to smell you all the time, I'm super used to it. And when I'm not in heat myself, it's mostly easy to ignore. So, you know, that's pretty much all the time when I'm not fucking up my medication. So I'm sorry."

"Don't worry about it." Then, on a half-mad impulse, Carlton said, "Make it up to me?"

"Huh?"

"I haven't been on a date since I moved here. How do you feel about buying me dinner? We can go to the barcade if you like. Buy me a pizza and beat me at skee-ball again."

Tony blinked at him. "Wait... *What?*"

"I'm asking you out. You can say no. It's fine. You got a girlfriend or something?"

"Uh... No... I, er, broke up with my boyfriend a couple of months ago."

"I've been single for a while. It'd be fun. No further strings attached."

Tony stared at Carlton for a minute longer. Then that mercurial grin flashed across his face and he said, "Sure! Sounds like fun. I will totally pay for the pizza, and the beer too. And I will totally kill you at skee-ball."

"Fine by me. Maybe you can let me reclaim my honor at one of the other games. I used to play a pretty mean game of original Street Fighter, back in the day. I think they've got one of those there."

"Sounds like a date," said Tony. "Friday?"

"Friday. See you there."

•   •   •

Carlton stepped inside the familiar barcade. It was alive with light and noise, as always. Friday nights were busy even when the boss wasn't there sponsoring happy hour.

He was wearing the same sort of nice button-down he usually wore to work, just one without a company logo. He'd dithered while dressing for a while, considering something fancier, but in the end it was skee-ball and pizza, even if he'd also used the word "date" to describe it, so he figured a suit, even a sports coat, would still be too much.

Carlton looked around and didn't see Tony. He went and sat at a table by the skee-ball machine, and tried to not give too much credence to the butterflies breeding in his stomach.

He shouldn't be nervous. He'd dated a lot in college, and at his first job after, too, though not usually coworkers. Hell, he'd dated a fair bit back in high school! Just it had always been women, and as far as he'd known, beta women.

Not that you could tell people's ranks just by looking, and plenty of omegas were quiet about it. So maybe he had dated one, and just hadn't gotten close enough to find out. He sure as hell had never dated a man before, omega or no, though.

He was telling himself to calm down, it was only skee-ball and pizza, just like a million after work happy hours, when Tony stepped inside.

Carlton felt a weird little flash of relief to see Tony in a casual polo too. He waved Tony over, and the other man dropped down to sit opposite him. "Hey there. How's it hanging?"

Carlton snort-laughed. "How's it hanging?"

Tony grinned. "Figured I'd better put you at ease."

"Hah. Well thanks, I guess. Shall I go order some food?"

"Nah, I'll take care of it. I'm treating you, after all." He gave a deliberate wink. "Gotta get back some of my alpha cred."

Carlton stared at Tony for a moment, then laughed. "Yeah, of course. Gotta be the man. I want a slice of the Greek, and whatever Belgian they've got on tap."

"One crime of a pizza and one absolutely omega drink, coming up," said Tony.

Carlton rolled his eyes, but he was still laughing.

Tony came back over carrying the two drinks. He handed Carlton his. "Now I have an IPA, a real alpha man's beer."

"You have so much hops you can't even tell it's a beer. It could be hopped horse piss, it'd taste the same." Carlton grinned and took a swig.

Tony laughed. "Touche. Anyway, they said the pizza would be a bit, they didn't have a greek up. So, want to go take care of the 'I beat your ass at skee-ball' part of this date?"

"Sure." Carlton rose, taking the beer with him, and braced himself for defeat.

•　　•　　•

"Hey, that one was only a hundred points less. You're learning!"

Carlton laughed at the blinking score, and at the cheerful Tony. "You're drunk, that's all. Your last score was dismal, come on! Admit it!"

"Okay, it was dismal. So hey, you've almost reached 'dismal', congrats!"

"Woo hoo!" Carlton pumped his fist in mock victory.

"Alas, I'm all out of quarters. And prooobably shouldn't have another beer. That was four. Four! Fooour."

"God, you are so drunk. Yeah. Me too. Probably no more beer. Definitely no more pizza. And I got no quarters either. I guess it's a night?" Carlton found himself strangely reluctant to say that. He'd had a really good time. He already knew he liked Tony in a friendly sort of way, of course. But it was different when it was the two of them, focused entirely on each other, and not mingling with other coworkers. Focusing entirely on Tony had been way too easy.

"Aww, man. But yeah, I guess we're done here."

"Want me to call a couple of cabs?"

Tony gave Carlton a rather frank up and down look, and then said, "I want you to call just one, for both of us, back to my place. Or to your place, I'm not picky. Is it nice? Mine's tiny, but I'm not a slob, I promise."

Carlton blinked at Tony. "Oh no. You're way too drunk. We're not doing that. Nope. No taking drunken advantage."

Tony giggled. "You're no fun. But no, no, totally a good idea. No drunken advantage. Come home with me, sober up, I'll make you breakfast and take sober advantage in the morning. I have a nice couch!"

"Tony…" Carlton hesitated. Tony was *definitely* too drunk.

"Hey, no, it's okay. You can say no. Proper consent, all that, it's all good. But seriously, couch is yours if you want it."

Carlton looked at Tony again. Then, almost to his own surprise, he said, "Sure. Might as well save on cab fare. How far's your place? Mine's only about three miles."

"Victory again! Yes!" Tony laughed, leaning against Carlton. They hadn't really touched all night, despite how close they'd sometimes gotten, and Carlton was intensely aware of Tony's body against his side. He swallowed hard, feeling a twitch of desire that had nothing whatsoever to do with pheromones.

Tony nearly fell asleep on Carlton's shoulder in the Uber. He woke up enough to drowsily protest when Carlton paid, but Carlton waved him off, and then let Tony lean on him again as they both stumbled up the stairs to Carlton's apartment.

Carlton managed to fumble the lock open and they both got inside still upright, which he figured was doing pretty well. No sooner had he shut the door, though, then he was practically pounced on by Tony, who pushed him up against the door, and before Carlton knew what was going on, Tony was kissing him hard.

Heart pounding, Carlton froze, not knowing what to do, and Tony immediately pulled back. "Sorry. Damn. Sorry. Just… Been thinking about that for a while."

"No, it's fine. It's…very fine. You just surprised me." Carlton reached out and pulled Tony in close, bending his head and offering a kiss of his own.

Tony gave a little laugh and kissed Carlton back, more gently this time, but still with passion to spare, molding his body against Carlton's as he did, pushing him back against the door.

This time Carlton had the presence of mind to wrap his arms around Tony and hold him, but it was definitely Tony driving things. When Tony finally broke off the kiss, Carlton was completely breathless with it. Not because he couldn't breathe, he had no idea where that came from in the things he'd read. Kissing didn't prevent breathing. But because his heart was pounding and he wanted to pant and gasp, he was so wound up. Kissing Tony had been intense.

"God. I've been wanting to do that to you since… Well, probably since I first saw you, to be honest. Definitely since you cornered me in that pantry, though."

Carlton blinked. "But… You were mad at me for that!"

Tony laughed. "Sure, because you were just doing it because of the damn pheromones. But there aren't any of those floating around tonight, are there? And because you were the one pinning me down. I *hate* that. Just because I'm short doesn't mean I want to be manhandled." He gave Carlton a look.

Carlton looked back, feeling startled. "Uh. Right, duly noted, no manhandling."

"Well… Maybe a *little* manhandling now and again. But only when I ask for it. I told you, the first time we met. I'm on top of everything I do. That includes relationships. If you can't handle that, I can just get my own cab home."

"Woah, no." Carlton held his hands up defensively. "I mean, you can if you need to, but that's fine, that's just fine. I'm not going to get into some kind of uh… Of…" Carlton tripped over what he'd been about to say.

"Some kind of alpha fight?" Tony grinned.

"Well, yeah. I never liked it, when other alphas got like that. It was so goddamn stupid."

"Yeah. Also stupid, though, is the idea that I'm some kind of submissive or something, just because I'm an omega. That isn't how I roll."

Carlton chuckled. "I'd noticed. Honestly, the confidence is pretty hot."

Tony grinned. "Oh good." He gave Carlton another quick, hard kiss. "I'm still pretty tipsy though. Man. I said no taking drunken advantage, so I better stop now. You got a couch or something?"

"Yeah, sure, although I can—"

Tony cut him off. "Nope! No chivalrously taking the couch. I'm shorter, I fit on couches better. You take the bed, I take the couch, we both get a good night's sleep, and we see what we feel like in the morning. Okay?"

Carlton blinked at Tony. "Okay."

"Good. You got a spare toothbrush or anything?"

"Ah… Sure, yes, here, I'll show you around."

Carlton got Tony settled in, with teeth brushed and with him dressed in a pair of pajama pants that were lucky to have a drawstring, since otherwise they'd have just fallen off of him.

Then Carlton climbed into his own bed. He was still a little drunk, so sleep tugged at him, but his mind took some time to quiet as he turned over the evening's events. It was all very strange and surreal, but he found he was happy about everything, from the date itself to the kiss after.

He hadn't even minded Tony pushing him up against the wall like that. In truth he'd always had a bit of a thing for, well, dominant sorts of women. At least in porn. Transferring that to a man—and an omega man at that, which porn had always presented as abjectly submissive—felt a little strange, and yet the memory of the way Tony's hands, smaller than Carlton's own certainly, but still very strong, had pushed him against the door and the forceful way Tony had kissed him ran over and over in his mind, and it was a very pleasant replaying.

·   ·   ·

"Good morning, beautiful."

Carlton blinked awake slowly. He'd never been a morning person. It couldn't be that early, he felt only vaguely hung over, and like he'd slept enough, but his brain wasn't working quite yet.

"Huh?"

Tony's laughter rang through Carlton's bedroom, and Carlton started to slowly process what had happened last night.

Oh.

"I thought I might make some breakfast. I noticed you had eggs to start with. Omelet?"

"Uh. Sure." Carlton stretched. "Though first, coffee."

Tony laughed again. "I'll make some for you. Sugar? Cream?"

"Cream yes, sugar no. And thanks."

Carlton eventually managed to scrape himself up out of the bed and shamble into the kitchen. It wasn't a very big kitchen, so he sat down at the little table in the dining nook and watched Tony move around. It wasn't Tony's kitchen, but he'd obviously explored it and claimed it as his own, for he moved about it with almost no hesitation.

"Here you go." Tony plopped a steaming cup in front of Carlton, and he took a sip. It was, of course, perfect.

"Damn. How are you so good?"

Tony just laughed. Then next thing Carlton knew Tony was bending over and pressing a kiss on him. Tony's fingers tangled in Carlton's hair, urging his head around just so, and Carlton felt an odd shiver go through him at that. Tony had claimed the kitchen, and Carlton felt like Tony was trying to claim him too.

Carlton was pretty sure he didn't mind.

When Tony was done kissing, he said, "Was that as good as the coffee?"

Carlton couldn't help but smile. "Yeah, I guess it was."

"Oh good." He looked over at the stove. "Pan's hot. It's omelet time!"

Carlton only laughed and watched as Tony continued cooking. The omelet was good, and it was delivered with another kiss before Tony sat down across the table to eat his own. "Seems like my 'taking sober advantage in the morning' plan is going okay," he said, between bites.

Carlton felt his cheeks turning suddenly red. "Er. Yeah, guess so."

Tony grinned. "Marvelous!" He inhaled the rest of his omelet, and Carlton had no trouble eating his either.

Then Tony was clearing away the plates, though Carlton did see that his perfection stopped short of doing the dishes, he only put them in the sink. Tony immediately came back over and got Carlton's head pulled up for another kiss.

God, it was good. Better than the omelet. Even better than the coffee.

Tony was suddenly in Carlton's lap, straddling the bigger man in the kitchen chair, and making Carlton very glad he owned sturdy furniture. Tony's hands slid up Carlton's chest and his lips were on Carlton's again, and all Carlton could do was put his arms around Tony and kiss back.

Tony pressed close, enough that Carlton could feel the bulge of his erection through his ill-fitting pajama pants. Carlton was sure Tony could feel his too, since he was very definitely turned on. Hell.

With a low, evil chuckle Tony rocked his hips against Carlton's, which made Carlton gasp into the kiss.

Tony broke off the kiss and said, "Mmm. The taking advantage is *definitely* going well."

"Hah. Yeah." Carlton was more than a little breathless, and had no idea what else to say.

Tony ground his hips down again and laughed at the sound Carlton made. Carlton couldn't help it, he was pretty wound up.

Then Tony climbed off Carlton's lap and held his hand out. "Care to show me around your bedroom? Especially the bed part? Preferably with you in it?"

Carlton swallowed hard, but took Tony's hand and let Tony pull him up out of the chair. Carlton had to do some getting up himself, given their relative sizes, but he wasn't going to complain.

The butterflies were back, though, as Tony towed him into the bedroom. Tony halted in front of the bed and looked back at Carlton.

Some of that nervousness must have shown on Carlton's face, for Tony said, more softly, "Hey, you okay? You don't have to do anything here. I can just give you another kiss and get my ass out of your place if you want. Or whatever else. I'm not going to push you."

Carlton shook his head. "It's not… I mean… I just haven't ever, er…"

Tony arched an eyebrow. "You can't be saying you're a virgin."

"No, not that. Just, I've never been with another guy."

His face broke into a warm smile, not his usual cocky grin, and he said, "Oh Carlton. I could just about declare my undying love for that. Not 'am omega' just 'another guy.'"

"Yeah, well." Carlton gave a little shrug. "I have some… thoughts about being with an omega. But that's not… That's not what I'm thinking about now. I just feel a little nervous. I mean, what the hell am I even doing? I don't know. I feel like I'm going to fuck it up."

Tony reached up and gently cupped Carlton's cheek. "It's fine. You know I'm a take charge guy. I'll just take charge. That okay with you?"

"Yeah." Carlton nodded instantly. "Yeah, that's just fine."

The cocky grin reappeared, and Tony said, "It's fine by me, too."

"Okay. So… Uh…"

"Let's get that shirt off. And the pants too, I think." He was pretty smug about ordering Carlton around. Carlton felt his cheeks heat, but he didn't mind. He pulled the comfortable t-shirt he'd slept in off, then shed the drawstring pants too, standing in just the boxer-briefs he'd worn under it. The effects of all the grinding and kissing earlier were very obviously evident in the way those were tented up, and Tony licked his lips, looking Carlton up and down.

"Very nice."

"Uh. Thanks." Carlton blushed even more, but Tony only kept smiling. He pulled off his own shirt and shed the borrowed pants. Carlton had already noticed how fit Tony was, and now he could see every muscular line of him. He too was showing a notable bulge in his briefs.

Carlton found himself staring openly as Tony peeled those off too. He'd never seen an omega man nude before. Of course he'd watched omega porn, and he'd seen pictures in sex-ed classes in school. Still, there was something fascinating about finally seeing one for real.

It was silly, of course. Tony didn't look that different from Carlton himself. His cock was smaller, and of course it didn't have balls, but it was otherwise exactly like any other cock. The other differences weren't especially obvious.

The view was definitely enticing, though, and Carlton found himself licking his lips.

"Like what you see, big boy?" Tony struck a pose, flexing, and Carlton laughed.

"Yeah, I think I do."

"That's good." Tony stepped in suddenly and gave Carlton a shove, pushing him back onto the bed. Carlton didn't resist, he let himself be pushed over, and willingly scooted back to lie on his back there.

Tony immediately straddled him, sitting atop his thighs, and ran a hand over the bulge in Carlton's boxers.

"Fuck." Carlton hadn't meant to let out that exclamation, but he couldn't help himself. Tony's touch felt amazing.

Tony laughed, but it was a soft, delighted laugh, not a mocking laugh. He cupped his hand over Carlton's cock, stroking it slowly through the thin fabric. "Ready to let me play with this, big boy?"

"Yeah," was all Carlton could manage. He felt like his brain was mush, but in a good way.

Tony stroked it some more, fondling and caressing, rubbing his fingers over the head repeatedly. Carlton clenched his teeth on a whimper. It felt good, but he wanted—needed—more.

"Don't hold back. I like it when guys react to what I'm doing. Let me hear you." Tony stroked over the head of Carlton's cock again. Carlton had one or two butterflies still hanging on, making him feel self-conscious, but he nevertheless allowed a whimper of pure need to escape him. It was all too easy to, as Tony continued to tease him.

"There you go. God, this is great." Tony ground his hips against Carlton, rubbing their cocks together, separated only by the thin and increasingly damp fabric of Carlton's underpants. Tony drew in a deep breath. "Oh yeah. You smell amazing."

Suddenly he climbed off of Carlton to kneel beside him on the bed. It wasn't really big enough for the both of them, but that was the last thing on Carlton's mind right now. Tony's fingers tugged at the waistband of Carlton's boxer-briefs, as he said, "Let's get those off."

Carlton eagerly helped, his cock springing free at last, and he hadn't even finished kicking the discarded garment off of his feet when Tony was straddling him again, skin to skin now, Tony's smaller cock rubbing against his large one. Carlton drew in a sharp breath, and let it out as a helpless moan. He was so hard it ached, pre leaking freely from him, and as Tony humped against him all he wanted was more.

"Tony," he managed, then trailed off, unable to form the words. He wanted to beg. He wanted to ask for all kinds of things. But his mind wouldn't come together. What should he say? Would it be the wrong thing?

"You want me?" said Tony.

"Yeah. Please."

Carlton hadn't meant to put "please" in there, but it had slipped out, and Tony said, "Oh yeah. You're going to have me, then."

Next thing Carlton knew, Tony was lifting himself up, his hand on Carlton's cock, positioning it beneath him. He paused only a moment before he started to sink down, taking Carlton's cock inside him. Carlton let out a groan of pure pleasure. The slick heat of Tony closing over his cock was amazing.

"Fuck." Tony's voice was suddenly ragged, his breath fast. "Fuck, you're huge. God." He had his head tipped back as he continued to slowly sink down, rocking his hips, taking Carlton's cock just a little bit deeper with each motion.

Finally he thrust down that last millimeter, and rested there, panting. Carlton let out another groan, completely lost already. He couldn't think of anything, all he could do was feel Tony's tight heat enveloping him.

Tony leaned forward, bending to give Carlton a hard, hot kiss. Carlton moaned into the kiss, eyes closed, opening his mouth willingly to Tony's insistent tongue.

Then Tony sat back, putting both hands on Carlton's chest, as if to pin him down, and began to move.

"Ah... Oh, god, yes," groaned Carlton, finally daring to rest his hands on Tony's hips and grip them as the smaller man began to ride him. He didn't pull down, that seemed like it would be taking some kind of liberty, but he couldn't keep from digging his fingers in as Tony moved on his cock. He was nearly there already, his breath fast and ragged, body tensed as he felt the pleasure building.

"God, you feel amazing," said Tony, still breathless as well. He thrust himself down in a swift, hard stroke that made Carlton moan again, then ground down on Carlton, taking Carlton's cock as deeply as possible. "Now let's make it even better for me, hmm? Here." Tony took one of Carlton's hands and moved it from his hip to his cock. Carlton unthinkingly curled his fingers around the hot member. His hand enveloped it completely, and Tony said, "Ah yeah, that's it. Good boy. Now stroke it."

Carlton gave a half-dazed nod and did so, squeezing and stroking, feeling the dampness of Tony's pre coating his fingers as he did.

"God, yes. That's perfect. Just do that a little longer." Tony started moving again, rocking on Carlton's cock but seeming to concentrate more on thrusting into his hand. Carlton felt himself shuddering near the edge, but kept his focus on stroking Tony, wanting to make the smaller man come first with an intensity that surprised him. He was almost desperate to see Tony's orgasm. He stroked faster, and gasped as he felt Tony clench down on him hard, the smaller man tensing.

"Oh, yeah... Getting close... God, you're so good. Such a good boy. Don't stop."

Carlton was beyond words, he just concentrated on the motion of his hand, still feeling that he himself was on the very edge, the way Tony was clamped around him, legs tightly gripping, inner walls squeezing as he moved, and yet so focused on Tony's pleasure that he himself couldn't quite tip over the edge.

Tony was panting hard now. He tipped his head back, tensing even further, and then with a gasp of, "Oh, yes!" he made a series of jerky thrusts into Carlton's hand and came, hot, milky fluid pumping out across Carlton's belly and chest. Spurt after spurt of it painted Carlton, and he felt a strangely intense sense of release to see it. He'd pleased Tony, he'd gotten what he wanted, and he was almost startled when, after a few breaths, Tony started moving atop him again.

"Your turn now, big boy. Come on."

"Ah…" Carlton shuddered, letting his hands fall, stained fingers finding a grip in the blankets as he finally stopped holding back. He lifted his hips, thrusting into Tony as Tony thrust down onto him, and it took only seconds for him to reach his peak. With a low, primal groan he came hard, cock shuddering, hips jerking convulsively as he emptied himself into Tony. It seemed to go on forever, pure, physical pleasure blanking his mind and thick, hot cum pumping out of him into his smaller lover, who was clenched hard on him again.

"Fuck, yeah," said Tony, when the last drops had filled him. He tipped his head back again, letting out a long, contented sigh. Then he bent over and kissed Carlton warmly, the motion shifting things such that a gooey mess flooded over both them and the bed. Carlton could hardly complain, he was messy enough already, anyway. Though he felt a vague puzzlement. He hadn't knotted. He'd been with an omega and hadn't. He tried to puzzle through why not, but his brain still wasn't in gear. There was probably a reason…

"You look like you're thinking something hard." Tony chuckled, though there was a wariness to his voice as he added, "No regrets, I hope?"

"No, hell no! That was great. Just… No knot still."

"Oh! Ha ha. Man, you need to watch less porn. I'm not in heat. Knotting is a heat response."

"Oh. Oh, right. I knew that." Carlton felt vaguely embarrassed, but only vaguely. He was still feeling too good.

Tony chuckled again. "No worries. Maybe someday. I wouldn't go into heat for just anyone, but... Maybe someday." He bent and kissed Carlton again, almost gently this time. "But come on. We're both a mess. I presume your shower works?"

"Yeah." Carlton tried to not sigh in regret as Tony climbed off of him. There was a further flood of cooling cum everywhere, but the sigh wasn't for the mess, it was for the absence of that wonderful warmth around him.

As he turned on the shower, Carlton found himself thinking that Tony fit him better than any lover he'd ever had, and he could almost give credence to the idea that an alpha/omega match was the "true" natural human pairing. But then, if the people who insisted on that were right, things would have gone very differently today, since those people also usually insisted that omegas were passive and submissive. Tony was neither of those things, and as far as Carlton was concerned that was just perfect. Everything about this morning had been just perfect.

He felt Tony's arm go around his waist, and found that Tony had gone up on his toes to kiss Carlton's cheek. "You look happy," said Tony softly.

"Yeah. Yeah I am. This was great. You're great. Not just the sex. That too, but..." Carlton shrugged, not quite able to put it into words.

Tony smiled. "Glad you think so. I think you're pretty great, too. Dunno that I'm ready to make any grand declarations, but, well... I kinda like you. Never thought I'd find an alpha I really liked, to be honest. But maybe I have."

Carlton smiled, and on impulse he kissed the top of Tony's head. "Yeah. I kinda like you too."

They washed each other off, and Carlton found something weirdly satisfying in helping Tony scrub his back. He had a feeling he knew how all these pieces fit together, and it was something straight out of his wildest porno fantasies. He was all too aware that fantasies could let you down hard, but figuring all that out was something for another day. Today he was just going to enjoy things and not worry too much about what it meant.

Out of the shower and wrapped in a towel, and still looking impossibly hot, Tony pressed another soft kiss on Carlton. "Sadly I need to get my clothes on and head out now. I left this morning optimistically open, but this afternoon I've got some things I need to get done." He flashed Carlton a grin. "I'll see you on Monday, though."

Carlton blinked. Oh damn. "Yeah, see you Monday," he managed, but all the while Tony was dressing, his mind was working over an all-new problem. If the two of them were dating, how the hell were their co-workers going to react? The whole lot of them were already way too nosy about his alpha sex life. Should he try to hide their relationship? But how could he act like nothing had changed? It would be impossible. Damn.

Tony, now fully dressed, kissed Carlton one more time. "See you Monday, and also I think maybe it'll be your turn to pick up the tab at the barcade on Friday, hmm?"

Carlton kissed back, letting his worries go, and wrapped his arms tight around Tony. "Sure thing," he said. "Hell, maybe this time I'll even beat you at skee-ball."

"Not a chance in hell," laughed Tony. "I told you the first time we met, I'm on top of everything. Now you know how true it is!" And then with one more quick peck he was gone out the door.

A Good Drink

t was Tuesday night and the hotel bar was deserted. I dragged myself over to a bar stool and immediately had the full attention of one very bored bartender. Poor guy. I'm sure he was hoping for some business, but I only ordered a water. For just a second he shot me a look that was nearly hateful, but then he put on his professional face and poured me the water.

He slid it across the bar, and I got a much better look when I slid three singles back the other way. I could afford to tip well. Hell the savings I made by not drinking more than covered a pretty generous tip. I could pay for the nice hotel room—or most of it, at least—with the savings I made by not eating, too.

I'm a vampire, you see. It has its good points and its bad points, but for me it's just the way life is.

People look at me like I'm nuts if I say that, of course. They're thinking of Dracula, Lestat, or maybe Edward these days, depending on how bad their taste in literature is. Or maybe they take me for one of the fetish types you sometimes run into, but I'm none of the above. I'm just an average Joe who happens to need blood to survive.

Well, all right, not entirely average. I *was* an average Joe, back when this happened to me, in good ol' nineteen-thirty-nine, but I was already nearly thirty at the time, so I'm a bit north of a hundred years old now, and while there are humans that age, I'm in much better shape. I still look pretty much exactly the way I did on the day I died, so I've been about thirty for quite a while now. It's a pretty decent age to be, I don't usually get carded but nobody gets too upset if I happen to hit on a guy who's actually a quarter my age.

Oh yeah, I guess that's the other not-average thing about me. I'm as gay as the day is long, though they didn't call it "gay" back when I was human. We used to get called fruits and fairies, though if you were being polite, you'd say "temperamental" or just "that way." Honestly, it's been real nice watching people's attitudes towards that kind of thing change. Sure humanity has a ways to go yet, and there have been some hiccups along the way—I'm not all that pleased with some current trends, that's for sure—but I'll take the way things are now over the way they were when I was figuring this stuff out any day.

"Hey there." I hadn't heard anybody approaching over the music playing—my hearing is supernaturally good, sure, but a lot of the time that just means the background sounds seem louder—but somebody suddenly dropped down on a barstool two spots away from me. I got almost instantly hit in the nose with a wave of bloodsmell, and when I looked over I saw he had a bandage wrapped around his forearm, with a little spot of rust showing where the blood had soaked through. I felt my stomach twist. I hadn't fed in a while. I was so damn tired I'd put it off until later tonight. Now I was going to regret that decision, because the scent of this guy was going to drive me crazy the whole time he was there.

He was a little guy, nearly a head shorter than me and I'm tall, but not that tall. Skinny as heck, and looking to be about twenty-five, tops. He was sporting a hipster look, with those thick black glasses, a little bit of scruff, and a flannel shirt in an unlikely pastel plaid. Not bad, really. I'd always had a soft spot for skinny little guys, what they call "twinks" these days.

The bartender came over, asking the guy what he wanted.

"You know how to make an 'adios, motherfucker'?" he said.

I couldn't help but grin at the name. Cocktail names were always ridiculous in any era, it seemed.

The bartender shook his head, and the little guy said, "It's an ounce of gin, an ounce of white rum, an ounce of tequila, an ounce of vodka, an ounce and a half of blue curacao, two ounces of sweet and sour, pour over some ice, and if there's any room left in the glass you top it up with sprite."

The bartender's eyebrows went up. Mine did too. That was a hell of a lot of booze.

"It'll cost more than our regular cocktails," said the bartender cautiously.

"Yeah, I figured. I'm not broke."

The bartender gave him another look, but then nodded and started pulling out bottles.

The guy looked over at me, taking me in. I'm just over six foot, clean-shaven, a little on the thin side maybe but pretty fit, and with sandy brown hair in an unremarkable cut. I wore tan slacks and a button-down shirt that hit a spot acceptable for both the bar scene and the business world, trying to blend in rather than draw attention. I didn't wear glasses, though I had before my change. I didn't miss them. I gave him a look back, along with a smile and a friendly nod. "That's a lot of booze. You getting over a girl?"

"A lot of booze for a guy my size, you mean?" He flashed me a smile. "Don't worry, I can't have a Napoleon Complex, he wasn't actually short. The height thing was just British propaganda."

I chuckled. "I've heard that."

"Anyway, I'm getting over my girl getting under a girl. She's up in the hotel room, banging her girlfriend right now."

I blinked at him, trying to sort out how his girlfriend could have a girlfriend. "Sorry to hear that?"

"Nah, it's not like you're thinking. We're polyamorous, so I'm fine with her being with girls. Or guys. Same with me. We're both bi and we both date around." Just then the bartender slid his drink over. It was in a tall Collins glass, and didn't look like it had much soda in it at all. He sent a twenty back the other way and told the guy to keep the change. That got him a smile for his generosity, though given the price of drinks in a downtown hotel bar he probably hadn't overtipped *that* much.

The bartender had apparently decided that this was the kind of drink that needed a cherry skewed on a paper umbrella, which the guy plucked out and ate, sliding it off the toothpick with his tongue almost sensually. I tried not to stare, but there wasn't really anything else to look at here. I could still smell his blood, too, and it was even more distracting than the way he'd licked the cherry off. Then he lifted the drink and took a good, long pull on it. It was probably a third drained when he set it down with a sigh. "That's more like it."

"So... I'm an old-fashioned guy," I said, figuring the conversation would at least be a distraction from thinking about blood. "You're going to have to explain this, uh…"

"Polyamory?"

"Yeah. Many loves? You're mixing your Greek and your Latin there, though. Shouldn't it be multiamory? Or polyerosy?"

The guy shook his head with a smile. "I didn't name the movement. But it's pretty much just what it sounds like, whatever language you're using. It's the idea that people can love more than one. So my girlfriend can love this other girl, and still love me. I can love her, and also love whoever else I'm dating. Though I'm not seeing anybody else right now, I've been a little busy, haven't really had the time to date much lately. But anyway, I'm not jealous, not like that. I think it's great when my girl has somebody else, she's always so happy. I drove us both up here tonight specifically so she could get with this girl. They've been talking over the internet for months now, and had a date a couple of weeks ago when she came through our town, that went really well, or so I'm told."

"So I take it you're slugging that thing back because you'd rather be out with somebody else than alone while your chick gets some?"

"That and the fact that I get a vibe that this girl's bad news. I'm not going to tell Michelle who she can see, that's a sure way to get her all antsy and defensive and then everything goes down the toilet. But Allison is just trouble. She was sniping at me every little chance she got, and I'm pretty sure she just wants to poach Michelle away from me. But they'll have to work that out between them, I'm not butting in." He took another swig of the drink, and I nodded and sipped at my water. It was a bit odd, but honestly I'd known people with weirder arrangements.

"I'm Tyler, by the way."

"Joe," I said, and held my hand out. I wasn't kidding when I said I was an average Joe, it's what my mother named me. Literally, she'd skipped the usual "Joseph" and just put "Joe" down when I was born.

"You drowning your sorrows too?"

"Nah, I'm just bored. I have nowhere to go and nothing to do, and I don't know the town well enough to find the night scene here. It's early for that kind of thing anyway, especially on a Tuesday." I gave a shrug. I had planned to hunt down a real bar, preferably a gay bar if

I could find one, later on, but right now I'd just been relaxing before dealing with the night that lay before me.

"Mister old fashioned likes clubbing?" He gave me a grin that just about had to be half caused by the steadily lowering level of his drink.

I shrugged. "I'm a better swing dancer than whatever they call what kids these days do at clubs." I flashed him a smile, though not too wide. I never smiled too wide in public. "But I'm old-fashioned, not dead, and clubs are good ways to meet people." Deciding that since he'd said he was bi, there was no harm in outing myself I added, "I was actually thinking of seeing if this town has a gay bar, though. Clubs are on the loud side for me."

His grin grew a little wider. "I see. Going out cruising, huh?"

"Something like that." Sex was very much the lesser of the two needs I'd be trying to fill, but getting close enough to get what I was really after tended to employ the same strategies.

"You know, I was in swing club in college for a few years. It's a lot of fun. I wonder…" He poured the last of his drink down his throat and got up, headed for the jukebox tucked into a corner of the bar. I watched him with some interest. He poked through the buttons for a while, then dropped in a couple of quarters and made a selection.

The drum intro to "Sing, Sing, Sing" is pretty unmistakable, though even before the music started I'd been pretty sure I'd be hearing *something* with a swing beat, given what we'd just been discussing.

"Here," he called out over the music, beckoning to me as he walked to an empty space between tables. "You said you did swing, right?"

I blinked across the room at him. "I only know how to lead," I said, blurting out the first objection that came to mind. He was definitely drunk if he was asking random men to swing dance in an empty bar.

"That's fine," said Tyler, still grinning. "I know how to follow. I was always the one who took the extra guy when we had odd numbers in swing club. Come on!"

I stared a little longer. Then I laughed suddenly. Maybe I wouldn't need to hit the gay bar after all. "Sure." I walked over to him and took his hand. I was a little rusty. I'd danced much more recently than when I'd first learned swing, but it had still been a few years since the last time. He really did follow beautifully, though, and it wasn't long before I felt confident in the basic moves, at least. His bandaged arm didn't seem to be bothering him any as we danced, either, he moved it as freely as the other.

The bartender looked at us both while polishing the bar, with the spot he needed to clean always in our direction, trying to not look like he was staring.

I started daring a few fancier steps, and Tyler followed them pretty well too. We had a few misses, any new couple dancing will, but I was having fun. He was too, and he didn't seem to mind one bit that the traditional moves were letting me put my hands all over him. They used to say that was scandalous, back when swing was new. It's funny how it's considered something conservative enough for church dances these days.

The song started to reach the end, and I dared try a dip. He fell into it trustingly, looking up at me with a smile that was both bright and warm, and when I pulled him back up and we stopped, with our faces just inches apart, I had to stomp on the sudden urge to go in for a kiss. That would probably be a little too fast.

He went for it instead. Just a quick little peck on my lips before he stepped out of my arms with a tipsy laugh, but I felt a shock of electricity from it. Damn but he was cute.

Tyler headed back for the bar and I tagged along. "My night appears to be looking up!" he said to the bartender as he took up a stool. I noticed he'd sat in the one that had been between us earlier. I took the hint and returned to my previous seat, which put him right next to me. I gave the bartender a glance, half-expecting a look of disgust or disapproval—this wasn't a gay bar, after all—but his expression was more amused than anything else.

"Here, make me another one of those," said Tyler, gesturing at his empty glass. I picked up my water on the rocks and sipped it, while giving Tyler a side-eye. One of those things had seemed like plenty.

He noticed my side-eye and smiled. "I've got all night to kill, so I'll nurse this one while we chat. Assuming you don't have anywhere to be?"

"Nope, nowhere but here." I leaned into him a little bit and let my arm brush his. "Guess I'll keep you company."

"What are you drinking, I can get you another if you like?"

I chuckled. "It's just water. I don't drink, actually."

He blinked at me. "You're an odd one."

"So people tell me."

"There any reason why you don't?"

"If you're asking if I'm going to start preaching about that monstrosity you're having," I said, as the bartender slid the second tall glass of bright blue over to him, "the answer is no. I got nothing against it. Booze just makes me sick, is all." I'd been there for prohibition, and it'd been one of the dumbest things the government had ever done—and there was a long line of dumb things to choose from. So I knew better than to try and tell somebody they shouldn't drink. I'd liked a good drink myself, back in the day, but of course I drank something else entirely now.

"That's a shame."

I shrugged. "I'm pretty used to it by now."

"So tell me about yourself," he said, taking a sip of the new drink.

I did, and it was mostly the truth, though I left the dates off of things. I could pick and choose among all the things I'd done to assemble a life that was at least worth discussing, and we chatted away while he drank. His idea of "nursing" his drink was to take a sip every minute or so, though, so it was less than an hour later when he'd finished the thing. He was quite definitely drunk, though for a guy his size he held his liquor pretty well. He wasn't slurring, he was just a little too talkative, his gestures a little too broad, his laugh a little too free. He was touchy too, putting his hand on my arm or slugging my shoulder, or just leaning in close as he talked. He didn't go for another kiss, but there was certainly some energy crackling between us.

I wasn't going to complain one bit about any of it, and I did my share of touching and flirting in return, even though I was dead sober. Emphasis on the "dead".

When he'd finished the last bright blue drop he pushed the glass back. "So, do you have a room here?"

He obviously knew what he wanted, but since it was what I wanted too, or at least adjacent to it, I wasn't going to argue. "I do, yes. Shall we?" I pushed back my own glass and slid off the stool.

"Let's!" His slide down was less graceful, but he walked more or less straight as he headed for the exit. I chuckled and took his arm, guiding him towards the elevators.

As soon as the doors slid shut on us he had his arms around me and was kissing me again. I kissed back hard, almost tempted to bite him then and there. I could still smell the blood scent coming off his bandaged arm, and I think if the ride had been longer I might have done it, but I was only on the fourth floor, so the doors slid open before I had time. The kiss was pretty damn good on its own, though, and he was breathless as we went out the elevator doors. I wasn't breathing at all, but he didn't seem to have noticed. Most people don't.

I led the way to my room and opened up the door, holding it for Tyler. He ducked in, then grabbed my hand and practically dragged me in after him. I laughed and let him while the door started to swing shut behind us. The door hadn't even finished swinging closed when he wrapped his arms around me and went for another kiss. He was pressing his whole body along mine, and I could tell he was already very much in a mood.

So was I, but the feel of my own hardening cock wasn't my first priority. The smell of his blood was still driving me crazy, and I couldn't hold back any longer. I broke off from the kiss to nip and nibble my way down to the side of his neck. He made a little sound of pleasure and tipped his head back, and that was all the invitation I needed. I bit down, sinking my fangs in quick and hard. I heard him gasp, felt him stiffen in my arms, but that was secondary to the wonderful, amazing, incredible taste of his blood as it welled up into my mouth.

Tyler relaxed suddenly, and I kept holding him up as he swooned against me, moaning. It took some guys like that, the sensation turning to pleasure instead of pain. I was just as glad, I didn't like hurting people if I didn't have to. That was all still secondary though as I drank from him, feeling the hot, heady rush of his blood fill the hungry ache at my core. That taste never grew old, no matter how often I had it down the years. It was rich and bright and better than anything I'd ever tasted while I was alive.

I drank deep, taking my fill from him as he moaned in my arms. I didn't worry too much about holding back. He was a little guy, but he was big enough to donate at the Red Cross, and I didn't usually take even a pint myself. A dizzying rush began to creep over me as I took in more and more, and I smiled to myself as I recognized it. Tyler was drunk enough that his blood in me was starting to make *me* drunk. I'd be less so than him, since I wasn't taking anywhere near half his blood, but he was pretty damn drunk and I got alcohol so seldom and in such small quantities that I was quite the lightweight. Not to mention the fact that it was going pretty much straight to my veins, without going through the usual process of digestion.

When I finally lifted my head, full to the brim, I kissed away the little trickles, swiftly slowing, that oozed from the side of his neck. My head was spinning pleasantly as I stepped back to give him a minute to process what had just happened. I was ready to deal with things if he reacted badly, making him forget all this was within my abilities, but I found myself hoping I wouldn't have to.

Tyler blinked at me for a while, his eyes glazed, his expression mildly confused. Eventually his eyes came back into focus again, and that focus was me. He blinked twice. "Uhm. That was...different."

I smiled, glad he wasn't freaking out. "It was, yes. You didn't seem to mind much, though."

"Mmm. No, I didn't." He blinked again. "You've got fangs."

I smiled a little more broadly, showing them. "Yes."

"So... You have a serious fetish and a really good dentist, or...?"

I chuckled. "I haven't seen a dentist in a long, long time."

"Holy shit." He blinked again, then suddenly stepped in and gave me another kiss. I let my arms fold back around him, pulling him close. "Vampires are really hot," he murmured against my lips.

"I'm glad you think so." I smiled and pulled back slightly from the kiss. "You should probably rest, though. You're pretty drunk, and probably extra light headed now. In the morning we—"

"Screw 'in the morning.' Well, then too if you like. But I want you right now, vampire Joe."

"I don't take advantage of drunk guys," I said, trying to disentangle myself from his suddenly clingy embrace.

"What do you call what you just did, hmm?"

"Survival," I said shortly. "That's different."

"Fair enough," he said, and he let me go. He was still looking at me with an expression of smiling determination, though. "But what if drunk guy wants to take advantage of you? Anyway, I'm not *that* drunk."

I gave him a look. "You're so damn drunk your blood is making *me* tipsy."

"Heh. That's a new one." His expression turned more serious and he said, "I'm a functional alcoholic. I drink like a fish and have a tolerance that would put an Irishman to shame. So no, I'm not that drunk."

"Oh."

"If I only fucked sober, I'd never fuck." He grinned suddenly. "I know you're probably from eighteen hundred or something, but you can stop trying to be a gentleman and screw me already."

"Nineteen-ten, actually," I said, and slid my arms back around him. "But if you insist."

"Holy shit. You're really a hundred and eight? Man, I bet after all this time you're really good at sex."

I chuckled. "I am lousy at blow-jobs. The fangs get in the way. But other than that I've seldom had any complaints."

"Well I hope you like getting them," said Tyler. Then he kissed me again, hard, grinding his whole body against mine as he did. His eagerness dissolved the last of my reluctance, and I kissed back with matching passion. My hands slid down his back, cupping his buttocks, pulling him tight to me. I could feel his erection, and I couldn't resist slipping my hand between us to grope him through the fabric of his tight jeans.

He returned the favor, and a moment later he was undoing the button on my slacks and had slipped his hand inside them to grope me more directly. I groaned at that. I was pretty keyed up, and I just about wanted to pin him against the wall and take him without further preamble.

It seemed he was in a similar mood, for next thing I knew he'd pulled my slacks down, and had my boxers down too. He didn't even give me time to step out of either before he had gone down to his knees with his hand wrapped around the base of my cock and his tongue working on the head of it.

I sucked in a sharp breath, partially in surprise but mostly in sheer pleasure as the feel of his tongue against my cock went through me in a wonderful rush. I let it out in a long moan and put my hand on the back of his head, encouraging him to continue.

He needed little encouragement. He was all over me, sinking down deep, then pulling back and letting his hand squeeze at the base of my cock. He lapped at me, took me in his mouth again, went down like somebody in a porn flick, working at my cock with almost frantic energy. It was the best damned thing. There's just something about a guy who's that eager to get all over you. It doesn't even matter that much how good he is, the eagerness is enough. But Tyler was pretty good, too. He obviously knew what he was doing.

"Fuck. I'm not going to last long if you keep that up," I said.

He pulled back just long enough to murmur, "Good," and then dove back down into my cock, taking all the way down his throat this time. God *damn* but he was good at this. His nose was right against my stomach, and while I'm no porn star, I'm not exactly small either, but he seemed to have no gag reflex whatsoever. His throat was working around me, tight and hot and wonderful, and I found myself fisting my hand in his hair, moaning as he worked on my cock. I was getting kinda weak in the knees, but I managed to stay upright as the pleasure built in me.

"Oh, god," I moaned, right on the edge. He made a humming sound of pleasure and intensified his attentions, and I couldn't hold back any longer even if I'd wanted to, I came hard. I felt him still swallowing around me as I did, and I groaned, my legs trembling. My hands ended up on his shoulders, bracing myself as pleasure shot through me and my seed shot out into his mouth.

He swallowed every drop, and when I was done he pulled his head back and grinned up at me. I managed to pull myself upright, though I was still wobbly. I took a step back and dropped down onto the bed, where I kicked off my shoes and got my pants off from around my ankles. "Wow. You are damn good at that."

"Thanks." Tyler just about tackled me with a kiss, he was obviously still keyed up. I kissed back happily, not minding the hint of my own seed in it. His hands were all over me and I was happy to get mine on him as well.

We rolled into the bed together, pulling each other's clothes off, and by the time that was done I was more than ready to go again. Tyler's enthusiasm was hot. So was his body. He was pretty skinny but there was enough muscle on him to keep him from being a total twig, and I enjoyed running my hands over every inch of him that I could. But of course I mostly wanted to get my hands on his cock. That was about average size, and uncut, which I always liked. He made all kinds of interesting sounds when I started stroking it, and next thing I knew he'd pulled me on top of him. He obviously knew what he liked. I ground my hips down on him, hearing him pant and moan under me. I gave him another kiss, and felt him run his tongue over my fangs. Remembering what he'd said about thinking vampires were hot I moved to nip at him, biting his ear and along his neck.

He sucked in a sharp breath, and I could hear his pulse going even faster than it had already been. His hands wrapped around me, nails digging in as he grabbed my shoulders and held me tight. His hips were lifting to mine, his cock rubbing against my own. I rocked my hips, rubbing against him, and bit him harder. I didn't need any more of his blood, and I didn't quite bite hard enough to draw any, but his reactions made it more than worth it all the same.

"Ah, fuck," he groaned as my fangs teased at him. I gave him one more hard nip, making him gasp, then sat back. My hand went back to his cock, stroking it firmly, and then I pulled mine against it as well, stroking them both together, feeling his hot hardness against my own. He tipped his head back on the pillows, panting hard and moaning repeatedly. His hands were still on my shoulders, and his nails dragged down my back. I let out a hiss of pain at that, but I wasn't going to complain, it felt great all the same.

I stroked both our cocks a little faster, my grip tight around them. He grabbed my head suddenly and pulled me down for another long, hard, hot kiss. "God, I want you in me right now," he said when he came up for air.

"Yeah," I said, feeling a little breathless myself. I didn't need to breathe, of course, but I was anyway, just to take in the scent of him— masculine musk and some kind of spicy cologne, no doubt something obscure and weird, given the hipster look he'd been rocking. I let our cocks go and climbed off of him to go fish around in my luggage for the condoms and lube I always packed. I didn't really need the former, I'm immune to STDs, so I'm as clean as it's possible to be, but a lotta guys are sensibly unwilling to have sex without them, so I always have some on hand.

Tyler picked a condom out of the box before I had a chance to and immediately tore it open. I didn't make any protest as he started to put it on me. He stroked firmly down my cock as he rolled it on, and I let out a groan and snatched up the lube bottle. I wanted to be in him just as eagerly as he wanted me there. He flashed me a grin and gave my cock one more squeeze, then laid himself down on the bed on his stomach.

I popped open the bottle and got a good puddle of the stuff. It was another thing I liked about the modern world, when I'd been having my first sexual experiences we'd mostly just used spit. Which admittedly I sometimes still liked to do when I was with a guy who liked it rough, but it was great to have better options easily available when I wanted them.

Now I lubed up my fingers and pushed a couple into Tyler's ass, spreading the lube around and stretching him out while I did so. He let out a moan, squirming around. I liked the sounds he made, it was always good to know you were having an effect. Guys who stay all quiet and don't react much aren't nearly as much fun.

I took a little time, working my fingers around in him, watching him writhe. "Oh god, yes," he moaned when I found just the right spot and stroked my fingers over his prostate. His hands were grabbing the bedcovers, his back arching, and he was panting so hard he was just about hyperventilating. I smiled and pulled my fingers out.

"You ready for me?" I asked, knowing the answer, but wanting to hear him ask for it all the same.

"Yes, god yes, please!"

His eagerness sent a pleasant shiver down my spine, and I swiftly lined myself up.

He moaned loudly as I started to push into him, and I couldn't help letting out a little noise of my own. His tight heat around me was really damn good. I kept going until I'd sunk in to the hilt, and then I ground down against him, pushing as deep as I possibly could. He moaned again, and there was a whimpering note in it that told me I was stretching him to the point of pain. He wasn't raising any objections though, in fact he pushed back onto me eagerly. That was almost as much of a rush as the physical sensation surrounding my cock. I found myself thinking that it was a crying shame that I'd probably never fuck him again after tonight.

Pushing that thought aside I got down to business, starting with a few slow strokes to make sure he was good and ready for me, and then bracing myself over him and taking him as hard and fast as I could.

"Ah! Fuck!" He writhed under me, his back arching, his shoulders all bunched up as he tensed, and I could feel him clenching down around my cock. I groaned and kept at it. After having come once already tonight I wasn't as on the edge as I might otherwise have been, but he felt incredible, and his reactions were an immense turn-on.

I decided to get a little more of them, and I bent over him, pressing close to his back, and bit the back of his neck, letting him feel my fangs. He cried out, a shudder going through him, and as I kept biting and nipping roughly at him his moans turned to a series of high-pitched, breathless cries that sounded like he was right on the edge himself.

Wanting to wring every drop of pleasure from him that I could, I slid my hand under his hips, finding his cock, and wrapping my fingers around it. That got a loud, low moan from him. It was hard as a rock in my hand, flushed and hot, and I could tell he was close. I stroked him as I kept pounding into him, and he grabbed the bedcovers again, his whole body tensed, just about screaming now. Then, with a loud, gasping, "Yes!" he came, hot cum spurting out over the bed under him and over my hand as well.

I stroked him through it, slowing my own pounding but not stopping, feeling an intense satisfaction at having brought him to that point.

He went limp under me as he finished and I halted, giving his cock one last squeeze and then letting go. He lay still for a long moment, panting, and I braced myself on my elbows over him, just listening to him, inhaling the scent of him, savoring the moment. I gave the back of his neck a nuzzle, and he made a soft, wordless sound of satisfaction.

Then I wiggled my hips, reminding him that my own cock was still there, still hard within him. He let out a long moan and clenched on me again. I took that as encouragement and I started thrusting into him again, seeking my own pleasure now rather than his. He didn't seem to mind that at all, he was soon moaning and writhing under me again. That only spurred me on and I slammed down into him until he was more or less bouncing off the bed with each stroke. I could feel it building in me again, and my strokes got irregular as I let go of all control and just took him, focused entirely on reaching my peak.

"Ah... Fuck... Ah, yes... Yes!" Suddenly I was there, streams of thick seed spilling out of me, that wonderful pleasure crashing over me, my body shaking with it as I emptied myself into him. A few more strokes as the last few spurts of it pumped out of me, as he moaned in deep satisfaction under me. Then it was past and I relaxed, laying atop him as a gentler glow of deep satisfaction washed over me. Feeling downright pleased with the whole world I nuzzled at the back of Tyler's neck and let out a long, contented sigh.

He echoed it, and we just lay there, still joined together. His breath slowed, and he made a little drowsy humming sound of contentment, sounding like he was more than half asleep.

Eventually my cock slipped from him, and I rolled off with a sigh of regret.

"Mmm. Thank you," he said as he rolled over and looked up at me, his face showing every bit of the drowsy contentment his voice had.

I smiled, feeling a pang as the thought that I'd probably never do this again recurred to me. Being what I was had its high points, but it had downsides too. "You're welcome."

He gave the bed a glance and said, "We should probably clean up some." I gave him a nod, and we spent a few minutes doing just that. When we'd done the best we could at that I half expected him to gather up his clothes and go, but instead he dropped back down to lie on the bed, still nude, and opened his arms in an obvious invitation.

Unable to resist that invitation I lay down and snuggled up to him, letting him fold his arms around me, and doing the same in turn. The warmth of his body against mine was good, and I just lay there soaking it in. I know I probably felt cool to him, but he didn't seem to mind. He turned to me and tucked his head under my chin, nuzzling up to my chest. I let out a long, regretful sigh and held him a little tighter.

"You mind if I stay the night?" he murmured against my chest.

I swallowed, almost wanting to just throw him out now so I wouldn't get any more attached than I already was. But after a long pause I found myself saying, "That'd be nice."

"Yeah, it would." He paused for just a second, then added, "So, you in the market for a boyfriend?"

It felt like a gut punch. I should have just thrown him out. "I can't," I said, and tried to not let my regret show in my voice, but I suspect I failed miserably.

"Not 'don't want to' but 'can't'?" He pulled back enough to tip his head back and look at me.

"Yeah. Sorry."

"Why not?"

I heaved a sigh and decided I might as well give him the truth. "Because of what I am. I've got to feed at least every couple of days, and it's a pretty...intimate act, even when I'm not cruising gay bars to find guys who'll let me close enough to have a bite. I can't bite any one person that often, I'd kill them. Red Cross actually makes you wait eight weeks between donating, you know that? That's a little over-cautious, but I can't take from one guy more often than once a month or so. So how could I have a boyfriend when I'm getting up close and personal with a whole crowd of different guys all the time?"

He actually laughed then, the sound bright and delighted. "Don't you remember why I was down in the bar in the first place?"

I blinked at him, then the pieces snapped together in my mind. "Your girlfriend's banging another chick."

"Yup. Polyamory, man. It's awesome. I would love to have a steady boyfriend, but if I did, he could go out and bang—or bite— whoever he likes as often as he wants to. So if that's your only objection to dating, I don't see why we couldn't give it a try."

"I…" I blinked at him, trying to sort my thoughts out. "I haven't gone steady in about eighty years. I suspect my expectations may be a little…dated."

He laughed again, a soft, amused chuckle. "When you're poly you have to talk about absolutely everything. How do you schedule your time so nobody you're seeing gets left out? Is everything up for grabs with anybody, or are some things off limits? Do you want to hear about the details when your lover fucks somebody else, or not? That kinda thing. So expectations aren't really a thing. Expectations trip people up, it's better to just ask for what you need and be honest about what you're able to give. Think you can manage that?"

I shook my head in astonishment, but I smiled while I was doing it. "Yeah, I guess I can."

"There we go then, boyfriend." He grinned at me, then went in for a kiss. It was sweeter than any of the previous kisses we'd shared, though there was still enough heat in it to make me almost want to consider trying for round three. I melted into it, kissing him back with tender warmth, pulling him in close as I did.

When he broke off the kiss he said, "So you can only bite me every month or so, right?"

"Yeah."

"I hope we can do the rest of this a little more often than that?"

I couldn't help but laugh. "Yes, yes we can."

"Oh good." Then he tucked his head back under my chin with a happy little sigh. I nuzzled the top of his head with a sigh of my own and hugged him tightly. As I cradled him close I couldn't help but think that I really did like this modern world, however strange it might sometimes be. I didn't know if things would work out, of course, but I was more than happy to have the chance to try.

Dare to Go A-Hunting

A very long time ago, and a very long ways away, there was a young prince named Byriam. His kingdom was a small, pleasant little place, taking up all of a lush, fertile, valley, whose river wound in an out among the barren desert hills that cupped it for miles before coming to the coast, where a small, pleasant city sat beside the harbor, with a small, pleasant palace on a hill overlooking it. Its people were by and large small, pleasant people also, and its history was mostly small and pleasant as well, for though it was prosperous enough in its own way, it had nothing to make anyone want to conquer it, and so it had escaped many of the wars that embroiled larger or richer kingdoms.

The king and queen were pleasant people as one might expect, but their eldest son Prince Byriam was bright and quick; full of both laughter and fire. He was also beautiful, in the way that young men can sometimes be beautiful, with soft, dark hair and soft, dark eyes in a fine-boned face with a strong, fierce nose and arched brows like raven's wings. His skin was bronzed by the sun, for he loved to hunt and be out and about in hill and valley, and his tall frame was made strong by that same love of action. All the unwed women in the kingdom swooned after him whenever he passed by, even sometimes the ones who were betrothed. Even sometimes ones who were wed after all, though they usually had the sense to swoon quietly and discreetly.

He laughed often, and shouted often, and lived his life far larger than someone in such a small, pleasant sort of place ought, so it was hardly any wonder that something far larger found him one day.

Prince Byriam was riding to the hunt, with his hunt-master and his hounds and a half-dozen young noblemen from the city who called themselves his friends, though none of them knew his true heart at all. Few did, the prince was not one for confiding in others.

He wore his fine hunting jacket of jade green doeskin and his fine riding boots of the same, with his sword at his side, his bow at his back, and a smile on his lips. He spurred his fine dapple-gray mare on over field and hill and up out of the valley, hunting wild boar but truly hunting nothing more than the chance to be out, riding, with the wind in his face.

The other young men rode at his side, joking and laughing with each other, and all in all it was a merry party as they rode past a great massif of golden sandstone that stood upon a hill near the nebulous borders of the little kingdom, out in the desert where nothing much was and nobody much went.

Such stones are in-between places, for their roots grow down to the bedrock and their tops reach up to the sky, so they bridge earth and air. As everyone knows, in-between places can also bridge worlds, letting creatures from the otherlands, the places where fairies and djins and other, stranger creatures dwell, reach into our own world.

It happened that just as Prince Byriam and his party were riding by the stone, Prince Safayid of the fair folk—who are sometimes called fairies and sometimes called elves—was riding by the other side of the stone, the side that existed in his own otherworldly kingdom, and heard the prince's laughter and the barking of the hounds. Curious about what the humans might be up to, he cast a spell to peer through the stone.

His eyes fell immediately on Prince Byriam and he was caught.

The fair folk can be flighty creatures—unsteady, unstable, and untrustworthy—but sometimes something sinks deep into the heart of an elven lad or lass and sets roots there, and when that happens they may never be entirely free of it. So it was that Prince Byriam's beauty, and his laughter, and the fire that flashed in his dark eyes sank deep into the heart of Prince Safayid, and the roots of it began to twine all through him.

He knew in that instant that he must find a way to make this human his own.

The fair folk can also be greedy and possessive, and they are not always kind or thoughtful about it. Yet what was twined about Safayid's heart in that instant was not only greed for the beautiful human boy, but love for the sound of his laughter and the fire in his eyes, and so the plan he laid in that moment was perhaps not entirely good, but it was not entirely cruel, either.

After the hunting party had passed, Safayid dismounted from his own steed, which was not exactly a horse, and sent it back to his stables. Then he invoked his magic, of change and illusion, and a moment later a creature that looked like a horse—though of course it was even less of one than his mount had been—stood on the otherworld side of the stone. Another flare of magic and he leaped through, his feet landing in the human world for the first time in more than a hundred years. He threw back his head and whinnied loudly, the sound carrying across the hills.

Prince Byriam's party were surprised when they heard the sound, and saw the wild stallion, but the horse was so beautiful, so perfect, that they all immediately set out in pursuit of it, without needing to consult and decide to do so. The elf-turned-horse had a coat like molten gold, bright and smooth and shining, with a mane and tail of pure white and hooves like bronze, while its eyes were obsidian-dark and striking. It was beautifully formed, like the fine horses of Arabia, with a compact, muscular body, almost dainty hooves, a wedge-shaped head, a narrow muzzle and delicate ears, but taller than most Arabian horses were. It reared and danced and ran like the wind, while the other horses, laden with their riders, tried their best to keep up. Prince Byriam knew in an instant that none of his horses could hope to catch the magnificent golden stallion.

Something in his heart sorrowed at that, for the horse was utterly wonderful, seeming like a piece of the strange, adventurous life he found little of in his small, pleasant home.

Yet to his surprise, after a hard but short chase the stallion ran down a dry wash that ended in an impassable wall, and was easily cornered there. Byriam got out a rope, making a lasso of it, preparing for a fight. The stallion reared again, dancing on its hind hooves. Byriam whirled the rope over his head and let it fly, and it flew true, dropping over the stallion's head.

As if aware that it was caught, the stallion instantly sank back to all four hooves and stood, calm, not even winded, despite the chase it had led them on. Startled, Byriam tugged on the rope, and the stallion came along calmly, as if the rope was a bridle and the stallion a lady's palfrey, not a wild creature held merely by a strand around its neck that it could likely shrug out of with hardly any effort.

His companions cheered and clapped him on the shoulder and praised him for his throw. He smiled and took their praise, yet he felt strangely shocked at how things had played out, and he kept running the chase and the moment over and over in his mind, looking for the cause of his astonishing luck.

Byriam was still somewhat in shock about having actually caught the fine stallion when he reached the palace, yet there it was, following docilely behind his dapple-gray mare. A servant came and took the mare, but he held onto the stallion's rope and led it into a stall himself, half afraid that if he let go of it, it would turn into a mirage and vanish.

He set about caring for it himself as well. The servants were mildly astonished, but then Byriam astonished everyone in the kingdom from time to time, so they soon adjusted to this new shock, and let him fetch the stallion a measure of oats, and get a curry comb to groom it with.

Standing in the spacious stall, amid the fresh straw laid down there, Byriam began to brush the stallion, working the curry comb over every taut muscle and every bit of shining, supple hide. The horse hardly needed grooming, it hadn't worked up the least bit of sweat, and the only dirt on it was a trace of dust from the road. Even its mane and tail were silky and smooth, as if it were groomed every day by an army of attentive stablehands.

"Is that why you were suddenly so tame, do you belong to somebody?" he mused as he cleaned dust and a few loose hairs from the horse's coat. "I suppose that wouldn't be surprising. Such a wonderful horse probably does have an owner. I hope they never miss you, or never find you, though. I want you all for my own. You're a fine stallion, and if I do keep you, I'll breed you to all my best mares. I'm sure they'd be pleased to be serviced by such a fine stud as you, and then I will get a whole crop of lovely foals."

The horse tossed its head and whinnied as if it was laughing, and something in the look it gave Byriam then seemed almost knowing. He left the stable feeling very strange about his new acquisition. It was a fine horse, but also an uncanny creature, and he was starting to wonder if it was exactly what it seemed.

•   •   •

The next day was St. Magnus' Day, and as he was the patron saint of the kingdom, there was always a great festival to celebrate. The king himself would ride in a procession, with all his children, and his lords and ladies would ride as well. So the palace was all a-bustle with preparations for the grand parade that morning.

Prince Byriam went to the stables right away and put a saddle and bridle on the magnificent golden stallion, which the horse accepted tamely. Byriam braided its mane and tail too, and the stable-boys gave him ribbons and flowers, which they had for all the horses, to be worked in among the braids. The prince himself was of course wearing his best coat, the long garment dyed with precious indigo dye and heavy with bright embroidery, over a fine silk shirt and pants of soft calfskin, with his very best black riding boots polished to a high shine. He looked a fine sight on the golden stallion as he rode it out into the stableyard to prepare for the parade.

Perhaps too fine a sight.

"What is this, son?" said his father as he came out into the stableyard. He was in his finery as well, and his embroidery was all of golden thread, even finer than the prince's. He was a bit like the prince, but his middle had gone to fat and if there had ever been any fire in his dark eyes, it had long since died. Instead a petty little gleam was there. He was a small man in mind, if not in body, and though Byriam loved him, he did not *like* him very much at all.

"This is the fine stallion I was telling you about at dinner," he said, reaching down to pat the horse's shoulder.

"He's fine indeed," said the king with a nod, but there was a look in his eye that Byriam didn't like one bit. "Finer than any other horse here, which means that he should be a king's mount, not a prince's."

Byriam tried not to scowl, he knew the expression only made him look like a child. He tried not to sigh, too, but only gave in to the inevitable and swung down out of the saddle. "I'll go have my gray mare saddled up then," he said, his voice resigned. A prince might usually get whatever he wanted, but not when the king wanted it instead.

"Good lad," said his father, and he put a foot in the stirrup. The stallion immediately shied away from him, tossing its head and whinnying.

"Woah there!" said the king, and he held tight to the reins until the stallion calmed. Keeping that grip, he got his foot in the stirrup this time and swung up, but he hadn't even settled in his seat when the stallion twisted and bucked, turning his swinging mount into a tumbling dismount off the other side of the horse, nearly head-first. The king's fall was broken by a hapless servant, so he came up unharmed and spitting mad. The servant soon was holding the reins tight and the king once again swung up red-faced and angry into the saddle, this time getting his seat properly. He nodded triumphant approval and told the servant to hand over the reins, at which point the stallion immediately started bucking like a demon, tearing them from the startled servant's hands. He bounced on all four hooves, then kicked out with his hind hooves, and then reared up, twisting and dancing, and the king came unseated despite his best attempts, and ended up on his rump on the hard flagstones. It was a well-padded rump, but his dignity was badly bruised, as was his backside.

"That horse of yours has a demon in him," snapped the king at Byriam.

Byriam tried not to laugh. "I'm sorry, father." The horse did laugh, tossing its head and whinnying.

"Never mind that. I'll ride my white charger. And if you've any sense you'll ride your gray mare after all."

Byriam nodded. He knew perfectly well that the king was right. Yet he couldn't resist the temptation. He went over to the stallion, who was standing still again, looking as calm and serene as if he hadn't just thrown a spectacular fit. Byriam took the reins, put a foot in the stirrup, and mounted up. The horse stayed rock steady beneath him. It didn't so much as flick an ear.

It was definitely an uncanny animal.

One with a particular fondness for him, it seemed. Byriam knew perfectly well that it was an absolutely terrible idea to ride the stallion. It was probably a terrible idea to even have it in the kingdom, he should no doubt be arranging to let it go or send it very far away. Yet he couldn't bring himself to do it. "I have no sense whatsoever," he murmured, and patted the stallion's shoulder again with a smile.

The stallion flicked its ears back towards him and whinnied another laugh.

It wasn't long before the parade was underway. Young men carried bright banners at the forefront, followed by a bevy of maidens who danced with scarves and strewed flowers in the parade's path, singing as they went. Their songs were sometimes hymns and sometimes traditional songs of the kingdom, and were all bright and cheerful, for this was a festive occasion, not a solemn one.

The king rode next, on a massive white gelding with heavy hooves, a horse that was trained in battle, though it had never been used in one. On a delicate white palfrey beside him came the queen, in a dress even heavier with embroidery than the king's coat, sitting side-saddle and letting her train fall over the horse's hindquarters. It trailed almost to the ground, trimmed with lace and little pearls.

The royal children came after. Byriam, the eldest, rode his magnificent stallion, and waved cheerfully to all as he passed. His younger siblings, three brothers and two sisters, rode beside him, most on sturdy ponies lead by servants, though the eldest sister was less than two years younger than Byriam, and she rode a fine palfrey of her own, with a coat of jet black, that made a handsome contrast to Byriam's golden stallion. She rode it astride, in a divided skirt, and laughed and waved also, for she had a bit of the same wild spark that burned so bright in her elder brother.

Then all the lords and ladies of the kingdom came, also on horseback, though the eldest were in open carriages decked with flowers. Behind them marched the royal guard, with pennons on their spears that flew gaily in the breeze off the harbor.

Behind them the city's children frolicked and laughed and darted out to pick up the flowers that had been strewn in the street, for it was held to be good luck to find a flower that hadn't been crushed by all the horses passing.

The procession wound its way from the palace down through the city streets and out towards the road that ran along the river, up the valley, and to lands beyond. A fair was set up at the edge of town, where there would be games and jousting and many other amusements for commoner and noble alike.

Just as the procession neared the fair, the golden stallion tossed its head and took off like a loosed arrow. Byriam nearly lost his seat in surprise. Thankfully he hadn't lost his grip on the reins, and he immediately hauled back as hard as he could, but that was when he discovered that the little head-toss had been the stallion settling the bit between its teeth, and there was no halting it now. In a flash it had raced past the king and queen, past the girls strewing their flowers and twirling their scarves, past the boys carrying their banners, and into the open road ahead. And then it *really* started to run.

Byriam yelped in surprise and bent over the horse's neck as the wind began to make his eyes water. It was all he could do now to stay low and keep his seat. The horse was going where it was going and there was no stopping it.

It rocketed down the road at an impossible pace, the fields and farms alongside it going by in a blur. Then it swerved abruptly and left the road. Byriam yelped in alarm and clung even more desperately to the saddle. Fortunately the horse slowed as it galloped through a field of newly planted wheat, but the ride didn't get any less alarming, for it was now having to leap over fences and hedges as it raced through the countryside.

Byriam soon recognized where the creature was headed. It was making a path towards the hills near where he'd found it in the first place. It left the well-watered farmland behind and galloped through the dry hills, until it came to one particular spot, where a game trail ran along the base of a huge massif of golden sandstone. Byriam knew the spot well. But the horse wasn't following the game trail around the huge standing stone. It was running on a trail of its own devising, straight as an arrow towards the stone's flat face. As it drew nearer it didn't slow, in fact it ran faster, and then its hooves left the ground in a leap directly at the massif.

The horse was going to break its neck, and Byriam's too, and yet somehow an instant later they weren't slamming into unyielding rock, they were landing, the horse's hooves thudding down on a carpet of rich green grass. It skidded to a halt and stood, breathing hard and a little bit lathered at last, though no wonder after such a run.

Then it gave a little hop and the stunned Byriam, who'd been so relieved at not dying that he'd let go his death-grip on the saddle, fell right out of it and tumbled onto the grass below.

He lay there blinking, trying to calm his racing pulse and gather his scattered wits. The world had just turned topsy-turvy, and it seemed it wasn't finished turning yet, for he heard a voice laughing, and looked up to see the horse vanished, and a young man standing in its place. "Ah, Prince Byriam. If you could see your own face just now! It is quite a sight. Hello and welcome to my kingdom. I'm Prince Safayid." The man held out his hand, and Byriam took it and allowed himself to be pulled to his feet.

Prince Safayid had fair skin with a hint of a golden tint to it, as if he might be as bronzed as Byriam if only he saw more of the sun. His eyes were jet black, deep and hard to read. His hair was as white as the horse's had been, and his face was as narrow, with a pointed chin and broad forehead, marked with arching eyebrows as white as his hair. His ears came to a point, if Byriam had needed to see further evidence that he was something other than merely human. A light coat of sweat sheened his brow, as if he had just been running very hard.

"You seem to have kidnapped me," said Byriam as he stood.

"It was not done in malice, I assure you," said Safayid, and something in his expression was hesitant, uncertain as he said it. Byriam felt puzzled by this. It was he who should be uncertain here, not the uncanny prince whose uncanny land this was. But he nodded acceptance and looked around him. The sandstone massif stood behind him, much the same as in his world, but ahead of him was not a dry desert, but a lush land of rolling green hills. One nearby was topped with a magnificent palace that had walled gardens and tended grounds spilling down the hillside below it and into the lower land around as well. A river wound around the hill, and a bridge arched over it, leading to a path paved in white marble that climbed up the hill to the palace's grand front gates.

"But come, you are my guest. Allow me to show you a proper welcome." The elven prince snapped his fingers, and suddenly a group of burly men with skin the color of old jade appeared, carrying a litter between them. They knelt, and Safayid climbed up to seat himself on the cushions strewn within the open-sided construction there. He beckoned, and Byriam joined him hesitantly. The cushions were comfortable indeed, but the space was very small, and he found himself sitting with Safayid's leg touching his, no matter how he settled himself.

The thought crossed his mind that the touch was not an unpleasant one. Byriam was one of those inclined as much towards men as women, and the elven prince was certainly handsome enough. He had been told that such things were a sin, but then riding too hard and laughing too loud were apparently also sins, so he'd had a great deal of difficulty believing in the notion of his own guilt on any such matters.

He knew someday he'd likely wed some nearby princess or influential court lady, but in the meantime he'd seen no reason to not take what joy he could, from man or woman. He took what joy he could from life in all things, whether it was good drink, or good food, or riding to the hunt, or bedding a pleasing partner.

He wondered if elves believed in sin.

Safayid's hand touched his arm lightly, and Byriam felt it as a shock, which went through his whole body, and seemed to set both his cheeks and certain parts of him much lower down aflame. He should not have let his mind wander to such things while so close to a handsome man. "Here, we are almost to my palace. You may consider everything within it yours, without question."

"That is generous treatment for a guest," said Byriam, trying to dismiss his blush.

Safayid only smiled, and the litter continued on, through the gates and into the gardens within, where fountains played and the paving stones seemed to be gemstones, for they were brightly colored and shone with hints of sparkling light beneath the sunlight. The litter halted before the palace proper, its bearers kneeling. Safayid alighted from it, and Byriam did as well. Three broad marble steps led up to the palace door, which was wide enough to drive a chariot through. It swung open as they mounted the stairs, though there was no servant manning it.

Inside was as grand and baroque as outside, everything lavishly decorated in rich materials; wood and ivory and stone. There were murals and mosaics and tapestries everywhere Byriam looked, and the floors were of perfectly fitting marble tiles, with hardly a seam between them, that sparkled in the light of a thousand candles in ornate candelabras and a thousand more lamps fitted everywhere on the walls. The whole place was impossibly sybaritic, and if he hadn't already known that he was no longer in the mortal world, he would have known it to see such things.

The high-arched hallway led to an even higher-arched dining room, with a long table that ran down the center, already laden with every possible kind of food. Byriam's stomach immediately growled, reminding him that he had been expecting a feast at the fair and thus had not even had his luncheon yet. He licked his lips and looked at the heavily-laden table, then glanced over at Safayid. "No offense to you, but I recall being told once that eating fairy food will doom you to never return home. I suppose I wouldn't miss the place immediately, but I don't want to be trapped here forever."

He was afraid that Safayid would be angry, but the elven prince only nodded. "I will swear whatever oath you ask that the food here is safe for you to eat. You are my guest, and I wish you to stay, but if you truly desire to leave, you may. I would not see you unhappy for all the world."

Byriam hesitated a moment, then decided that he might as well. This was the kind of grand adventure he'd thought never to have, and he wasn't going to starve himself when he could be eating every possible good thing under the sun. In any case, if Safayid wasn't trustworthy, then he was probably doomed anyway.

So he went to the table and dug in with a will, and Safayid sat beside him and ate also.

The food was good and the wine was even better, yet when Byriam was finally sated, he found that he felt only a little merry, not nearly as drunk, nor nearly as stuffed as he probably should be. Well, it was fairy food, and probably not to be trusted after all, but it was much too late for that.

"Does dinner meet with your satisfaction, Prince Byriam?"

"It does," said Byriam with a replete sigh.

"Then come, let me show you to where you may stay the night, if you wish."

Byriam nodded and rose, once again following his host through the baroque and lavish hallways, and up a grand flight of stairs, to a massive bedroom. It was as luxurious as everything else here, and the bed looked large enough to sleep half an army. It took up nearly half the enormous room.

"That is a very large bed," Byriam remarked, wondering if he was meant to actually sleep in it, or if it was something else entirely and merely covered in blankets and pillows so that it looked like a bed.

"It needs to be large enough so that all four of my wives can join me, when they are in residence," said Prince Safayid, and there was some of that strange uncertainty in his voice again as he spoke.

Blinking, Byriam looked over at him. "This is your bedchamber, then?"

"Yes."

"And you are married."

"Yes. Though the fair folk regard marriage differently from the way humans treat it. We live forever, or near enough to it. To spend forever tightly bound to only one person is...less than practical for most. So we take lovers often, and may marry more than one as well, and sometimes spend years, even centuries apart. I have seen my wives a few times of late, they get along well and often visit together, even, but they are not here tonight, nor are they likely to be here for some time."

"I see. And you have taken me to your bedchamber." Byriam felt absurd as soon as he said it. Of course Safayid had, they both knew that. He felt his cheeks flushing again.

"Yes," said Safayid softly. His cheeks seemed to bear a hint of pink as well. "As I said, only if you wish. There are other bedchambers here. I will show you to one, if you prefer it."

Byriam hesitated, looking at the elven prince. There was very little doubt what sort of invitation he was being offered. There was every possibility that accepting it was unwise. It was probably a sin, as well. Yet like riding the golden stallion in the procession, like eating the fairy food, like so many other things he'd done that were louder and larger and more reckless than those around him, Byriam couldn't shy away from this opportunity. So he smiled, and reached out to brush his fingers against the elven prince's arm, finding his skin warm and pleasant to the touch. "I would be honored to stay here," he said.

Safayid's face lit up like a child given a gift, and he smiled at Byriam in delight. "I am honored as well. Thank you!" He pulled the door shut behind him and strode into the room. "Consider everything here yours as well. There is a very fine bathing room, if you would like a bath?"

"That sounds good," said Byriam. He had worked up a sweat while clinging to the golden stallion that had been Safayid, and the dust of the road was always present as well. Not to mention that bathing was often a good way to lead smoothly into lovemaking. It was a less-awkward way of getting one's clothing off, certainly.

The bathing room was, of course, also impossibly luxurious. The tub was set into a kind of tiled platform, and was more than big enough for two. Byriam could nearly have swum in it. He found himself wondering if it was meant to fit all four wives as well. It probably could, though if Safayid joined them they would all have to be quite friendly.

That was a happy mental image. If elven women were as lovely as elven men handsome, they'd no doubt be good to look at.

He shook that thought aside and set about shedding his clothing. The tub was somehow already filled with fragrant water that steamed ever so slightly. Safayid stripped off the complicated, layered outfit of foreign cut—although perhaps it should be considered otherworldly cut?—he'd been wearing and stepped naked into the tub. Byriam saw that he was slender and very lean, his muscles moving smoothly beneath golden skin, everything about him graceful, almost delicate, from his long-fingered hands to the seashell tips of his pointed ears. Byriam noticed Safayid looking his own now-naked body over as well, and found himself blushing once more, but it was a pleasant sort of thing. He was fit himself, broad shouldered and well-muscled, and not the least ashamed to have his naked flesh on display. He knew perfectly well where this evening was going. The process of it going there would happen as it happened, and that was just fine.

The tub had a tiled bench inside it, and Safayid sank down to sit on it, the water coming up to his chest. Byriam joined him, enjoying the relaxing warmth as it closed over him. He sat close by, not quite touching, but very nearly, though there was room enough to be at arm's length.

"There are soaps and oils and such there," said the elven prince, gesturing at a shelf along the back of the tub, where jeweled boxes and elegant bottles of colored glass were lined up. "Choose whatever ones you like." Byriam rose to examine them, and eventually selected a soft soap that smelled of sandalwood. He began to scrub himself down with it, standing in the waist-deep water, but only a moment later the bar was plucked from his hands by a smiling Safayid. "Allow me."

Byriam blinked at him for a moment, then smiled back. "Of course."

"It's only courteous to help a guest," said Safayid.

Byriam chuckled. "You have been a paragon of courtesy thus far, your highness."

"Please, just call me Safayid."

"Then you must call me Byriam."

They smiled at one another, and then Safayid began soaping Byriam's skin, running the soft bar all over him, creating a gentle, fragrant lather, and rubbing it in with his hands. They were warm and strong, the long, elegant fingers giving a pleasant massage as they rubbed the soap over Byriam.

Safayid slid the bar beneath the water as well, and did not neglect to wash a single inch of Byriam's body. As the touches became more and more intimate, Byriam found himself breathing faster, and making soft sounds of pleasure. It felt very good indeed, even when—

especially when—the soap was finally discarded and Safayid simply ran his hand over where he had been washing just moments before, caressing Byriam's cock, which was already coming erect.

As he began to slowly stroke there, Safayid pressed close and gave Byriam a kiss. It was gentle, hesitant even, but as Byriam kissed back it became deeper, more passionate. Soon they were pressed tightly to each other, tongues twisted together as they kissed hotly. Safayid's hand continued its stroking too, though it was leisurely, in no hurry to reach any particular conclusion. Byriam appreciated that, and he let his own hand grope between Safayid's legs, finding the cock there and squeezing it in return.

A soft sound of pleasure escaped the elven prince as he pulled back from the kiss. Byriam smiled, stroking more firmly, and then, giving in to an urge that had been lurking somewhere in the back of his mind since he'd first seen them, he leaned in close and nibbled lightly at one of Safayid's long, pointed ears. It seemed to be quite sensitive, for despite the gentle care with which he closed his teeth over it, the elven prince sucked in a sharp breath. "Ah…"

"Is this well?" he murmured.

"More than," Safayid replied breathlessly.

"Mmm…" Byriam resumed, nipping from the lobe up to the delicate tip, and Safayid gasped and moaned softly with each touch of his teeth. His hand on Byriam's cock loosened as he was thoroughly distracted, but Byriam didn't mind. It was good to have a partner who reacted. Lovers who merely lay there and allowed one to go about it weren't much fun at all. Safayid's gasping and squirming as Byriam bit harder was much more fun.

He nipped sharply at the tip of Safayid's ear, and Safayid cried out, his hand finally dropping entirely as a shudder went through him. Byriam pulled back then and smiled at him, letting his own hand fall from Safayid's cock as well. Then Byriam wrapped his arms around Safayid and pressed a warm kiss on the elven prince. Next thing he knew he was being pressed back into the bench, with Safayid straddling his lap, kissing with fierce insistence as he ground their hips together. Byriam groaned softly into the kiss as he felt Safayid's cock rubbing against his beneath the water.

Safayid kept that up for a long, wonderful time, kissing deeply, hands caressing, bodies pressing and rubbing together, before he finally sat back and climbed off of Byriam. "I feel that I am clean now. And you?"

Byriam chuckled. "I do seem to be very clean. Scrubbed all over, in fact. You have been a most obliging host."

"It is a host's duty to see his guests' comfort." Safayid grinned. Then he climbed out of the tub, dripping on the tile floor, and reached for where several robes hung on a peg against the bathing room wall. He handed one to Byriam, who found it to be of thick cotton terry cloth, and wrapped it around himself. It dried him wonderfully. The scent of sandalwood lingered pleasantly on his skin as he followed Safayid out of the room and into the big bedroom.

The elven prince vaulted into the absurdly large bed and sprawled out on his back there. Byriam stood beside it, looking down at him, then smiled and climbed in. Byriam noticed that Safayid's bathrobe hadn't been belted and was falling open, revealing his firm chest and his still quite definitely erect cock. Byriam's eyes fastened on that and he licked his lips. He very much enjoyed a cock. As wonderful as being with a woman always was, there was just something about a man's member that was enthralling.

"You have been such a good host to me," he said and he climbed across the bed to where Safayid lay. "Yet I have neglected to bring my host a gift, as a polite guest should. Perhaps I can do you some small... service instead?" He smiled down at Safayid, who reached up and ran his fingers through Byriam's short, damp hair.

He pulled the human down for a short, intense kiss, then let him up again and said, "That seems like an excellent idea. Proper etiquette should be observed."

"Indeed. And I have just the service in mind." His fingers drew up the length of Safayid's cock in a light caress, and Safayid let out a long, blissful sigh at it. Byriam touched and stroked and explored the elven prince's member. As far as he could tell it was indistinguishable from a human man's. It was uncircumcised, which seemed obvious, since elves were quite unlikely to be Jewish, and was of a modest but pleasing size. It was flushed red, hard and hot in his hand, and it was a pure pleasure to bend his head and begin to lap at the tip. Safayid tasted of faint musk with a hint of sandalwood, and as Byriam lapped over the head of it he also tasted a salt-sweet drop of pre. That was good to him, and he set to work getting more, taking the head of Safayid's cock into his mouth and beginning to sink down on it.

Safayid moaned, and he put one hand on the back of Byriam's head, not pushing down, simply resting there, fingers caressing his hair. Byriam made a pleased, if rather muffled sound at the caress, and continued to sink lower. Safayid's cock was soon pressing at the back of his throat, but he was decently skilled at this and neither hesitated nor gagged at the feel of it.

"Ah, stars above," gasped Safayid softly, and his fingers twisted in Byriam's hair as Byriam took the full length of the elven prince's cock deep down his throat.

Byriam could make no reply, but he didn't mind. He was focused on his self-appointed task, working his tongue along Safayid's cock, swallowing around the tip of it as it filled his throat. He could only stay down for so long of course, but when he pulled back it was only to take in a swift breath before diving back down again. He set up a steady rhythm, working back and forth on the hard member, his eyes closed as he concentrated on pleasing his host.

Safayid moaned and gripped Byriam's hair more tightly. His body was tensed as his pleasure built, and a moment later Byriam tasted the musky, bitter-salt flavor of Safayid's seed, the elven prince's cock twitching and pulsing as he came into Byriam's mouth. Byriam swallowed it willingly, staying down on Safayid's cock, and feeling a warm rush of pleasure at having brought the other man to his peak.

When he'd gotten every drop, Byriam lifted his head and swallowed one last time. With a contented sigh he gave the head of Safayid's cock a final lick, then let his head fall to rest on Safayid's thigh. The elven prince sighed too, a deep, happy sound, and stroked Byriam's hair.

They rested together in comfortable silence for a long time. Eventually Byriam lifted his head and sat up. Safayid opened his arms in invitation, and Byriam pressed himself into that embrace, giving Safayid a gentle kiss.

"My beautiful, bright, and it seems extremely talented prince...
This is even better than I had imagined when I set out to lure you here,"
murmured Safayid.

Byriam chuckled. "I am very glad I was so lured. Though
I think it was a bit more like being kidnapped. I have no objections,
though. This has been delightful. I was pleased when I thought I'd
gotten a fine golden stallion. I am much more pleased to have gotten a
fine, handsome lover."

"Ah, but I am being a poor lover and a poor host now," said
Safayid with a smile, his arms still holding Byriam close. "I have had my
own pleasure, but what of yours?"

Byriam shrugged, saying, "I have never believed that one must
exchange pleasure the way one exchanges money for goods at the
market. I am content enough."

"But what if I am not content without pleasing you?"

Byriam chuckled again. "I suppose I would be an ungrateful
guest if I refused you, in that case. Do you want an equal exchange then?
Or would you rather do something else?"

"What I want," said Safayid, leaning close and whispering this
intensely in Byriam's ear, "is to have you inside me."

Byriam felt his breath catch, his heart suddenly beating faster.
He licked his lips and nodded, unable to find the words to reply with.
It seemed no words were needed, though, for Safayid pulled him close
and kissed him deeply. His earlier kisses had been warm, but this was
made of fire, heated with pure passion, and it thrilled through Byriam.
He pressed tightly to Safayid, and felt his suddenly renewed erection
pressing against the other man as desire filled him. He wanted precisely
what Safayid wanted, and *now*. So he was not at all disappointed when
Safayid broke off the kiss and pulled himself from Byriam's arms, for the
elven prince said, "Allow me to fetch some oil, to prepare myself with."

"Of course." Byriam sat and waited, with patience but also
anticipation, as Safayid went to a chest at the foot of the bed and dug
around in it for a moment, before returning with a beautiful blown-glass
bottle.

"Let me anoint you first," he said, smiling at Byriam, who smiled back and nodded. Safayid opened the bottle, pouring out some of the sweet-scented oil within into his hand. Then he reached out and began spreading it on Byriam's cock. Byriam made a soft sound of pleasure. The feel of Safayid's fingers against his aching cock was wonderful, but it only made him want more. Safayid caressed him thoroughly, his hand covering every inch of him, squeezing and stroking far more than strictly necessary. Eventually, though, he got a second little puddle of oil, and now he lay on his stomach on the bed, his legs spread apart, his back arched, and he pushed his own fingers within himself, spreading the oil there.

Watching this display, Byriam found himself licking his lips, his already aching cock becoming even harder, if that were even possible. He wanted Safayid badly.

Safayid looked back over his shoulder at Byriam. He didn't say anything, but he didn't need to, the desire in his eyes was clear. Byriam couldn't hold back one instant longer, he moved atop Safayid, bracing himself over the handsome elven prince, his heart pounding in anticipation. He lined his cock up with Safayid's entrance, and he felt Safayid panting beneath him as he did, obviously equally eager. "Come, my beautiful prince, take me as yours," said Safayid, his voice trembling.

"Yes," breathed Byriam, and he began to sink down into Safayid. He groaned as he thrust in further. The slick heat closing around him eased the ache he felt, but did not quench the fire, it only made it burn all the brighter. He sank in to the hilt, and Safayid beneath him moaned loudly when he came to rest.

"Ah... Sun and stars... You feel so good," he said.

"God, yes," replied Byriam, and he pulled back and thrust in again, making Safayid moan again. The sound was marvelous, and the feeling was marvelous, and Byriam gave up all other thought and lost himself in it, his hips bucking, thrusting deep and hard into Safayid.

"Ah!" The elven prince cried out, body arching beneath Byriam, his hands fisting in the bedcovers. The cry was definitely of passion, though, not of pain. Or if there was pain, the passion came with it. Safayid writhed and moaned and pushed back into each stroke, which only spurred Byriam on to take him all the harder. It was bliss, and need, and white-hot pleasure that built and built until finally it spiraled up to an unstoppable peak and with a low cry of utter fulfillment Byriam came hard, his seed spilling out into Safayid beneath him, pumping in deeply as he thrust in one last time.

Then the moment was past and Byriam relaxed, panting, a warm, contended glow seeping through him. Safayid was panting beneath him as well, and he let out a soft, happy sigh as he lay there under Byriam's warm weight.

The hearts of elves can be fickle, feckless things. They may use and discard a lover as easily as they use and discard a sword, or a harp, or any other plaything. Yet that is because they love seldom, for their lives are long, and their true hearts run deep. Those they seem to love and discard never truly took root there at all.

When love does take root in the heart of one of those fair folk, man or woman, it roots deeply, swiftly, and profoundly, and they are utterly lost to it. When Safayid had first seen Byriam, the tendrils of a fascination, affection, and desire that were very much like love had wrapped themselves instantly around his heart. Now, having met the prince, and spoken with him, and eaten with him, and made love to him, Safayid knew that Byriam was in truth everything he had seemed when the elven prince had first seen the fire in his dark eyes and heard him laugh.

So those entwining tendrils were transmuted from fascination to love, deep within him. And thus, when Byriam finally rolled from him to lie beside him, Safayid wrapped his arms around the human prince tightly, and kissed him sweetly, and said, "I love you, my beautiful, wonderful prince."

Byriam was not of the fair folk, and was just old enough, and just wise enough, to know that one should not give love in an instant. Yet something touched his heart also to hear those words. To say he loved the elvish prince would be wild, and reckless, and foolish in the extreme. Yet riding the golden stallion had been all those things. Eating the fairy food had been all those things. Making love to Safayid had been all those things. So, as they rested together, sated and warm in the soft twilight of otherland, Byriam said softly, "I love you too."

And in that moment, at least, it was true.

The Only Chance Inn

*T*humbed the switch of my bead gun from "off" to "sub1" and lifted the compact little weapon, squinting along the sights atop the barrel. I didn't have an implant, so I had to aim the old-fashioned way. Perhaps if this year was a good year I'd use some of my profits to finally get one. They weren't too expensive, but I'd have to visit civilization in order to have it installed, and taking the time off was always hard to do.

I pulled my thoughts back to my target and re-centered my aim. The beer bottle on the old fence post, fortunately, hadn't gone anywhere while my mind meandered. I squeezed the trigger, sending a little ceramic pellet shooting out the end of the gun with a distinct *paff!* It hit the bottle and knocked it over. The low-speed missile didn't carry enough energy to break the bottle. It was basically a children's toy, on that setting. I could recall my father letting me use a bead gun with the other settings locked off when I'd been about eight. With a smile I nudged the switch to "sub2" and took aim at the next bottle. This time the gun went *ping* at a high pitch instead of the low, soft *paff*. The bottle shattered into a satisfying shower of shards as the barely-subsonic pellet slammed into it.

I grinned and thumbed the switch again. The "super1" setting made the next bottle explode into tiny, glittering fragments with the force of its impact. The dense composite pellets were the same on any setting, but force equals mass times velocity, so upping the speed could make quite a difference in the results.

I lined up another bottle in the sights, and another flick of the switch to "super2" before firing resulted in the bottle jumping off, apparently intact. I lowered the weapon and walked across the sagebrush-strewn ground behind The Only Chance Inn, which I owned, to make certain that the faster setting had worked as it should. A neat hole was punched through the bottle, and I nodded in satisfaction.

One more shot. I walked back and drew imaginary cross-hairs on one final bottle. With the gun now set on "hyper" I fired one more time. The *ping* of the pellet being spat out the front of the gun was gone, the noise now too high to hear. The bottle seemed totally untouched, as if I'd missed. I walked over again and inspected it once more. Another satisfied smile crossed my face as I saw the neat hole, much like the previous one, but punched through so swiftly that the bottle hadn't even twitched. Rather like pulling the tablecloth out from under a set table, the high speed kept the energy from transferring.

Excellent. Everything was still in perfect working order. If for some ungodly reason I needed to shoot something with heavy armor, the hypersonic bead would be absolutely devastating.

"All done, Jack." I holstered the gun at my hip and resettled my hat on my head. I was dressed in the costume worn by working folks in this part of the world for centuries; a plain buttoned shirt, dark brown jeans, synth riding boots with low heels, and a broad-brimmed brown hat. The gun belt was of course part of the outfit too, in the same shade of brown as the hat. It was only a half shade darker than my tanned skin. My hair was jet black, and my eyes were a deep, chocolate brown. I figured I cut a pretty fine figure, and the lovers I'd had in the past seemed to agree.

"Very good, sir." The inhuman voice of the cleaning bot was primly accented entirely by Jack's choice, given that bots couldn't really have "natural" accents. He probably watched too many old holo-dramas; I was fairly certain the sentient machine thought of himself as a butler. Jack moved forward, trundling on his treads, his loosely human-shaped head swiveling to scan across the array of shattered glass and intact bottles. I gave him a pat as he passed by on his way to clean up the mess my target practice had caused.

I left the robot to his work and went inside the inn. The back door led to the kitchen, where another bot was bustling around over heating surfaces and cooling drawers, preparing for the dinner rush, such as it was.

The inn didn't get that much business. It was the only stop on the road from Eslesee to Vegas these days, unless you wanted to camp in an old ruin or stop in a hot crater and get irradiated, but most folks who made the trip were wealthy enough to do it in a hopjet, which took only half an hour or so. The poor mostly just didn't go. Long, long ago poor folk had lived all around here, farming, but open-air farming had long since been mostly replaced by vat-farms, and much of the land around here was hot, so crops would be too contaminated to use.

The kitchen led to the restaurant, which was currently empty, and from there I went to the inn's lobby and out into the dusty yard in front of the sprawling two-story building. There was room there to park all sorts of vehicles, including a hitching post with its accompanying watering trough. People in this part of the world had been using horses to get from here to there for thousands of years now. They were slower than ground cars or hover vehicles, but they could go over the rough patches where the road was breaking down, or off the road entirely, and they were self-fueling if you could find a stream or a seep with good browse along it. Even if you couldn't, hauling enough oats for the trip was more practical than hauling enough batteries for some vehicles.

Plenty of motor traffic could still make the trip, and I saw a hovercar zip past as I walked across the gravel parking lot. It was flying high, more energy intensive, but necessary over large portions of the road. I almost never saw groundcars, it was just too rough over large stretches for wheeled vehicles to make decent time. You'd need an off-roading setup and you'd go about as fast on horseback.

The thing hadn't been maintained in more than a hundred years, so the rough shape was understandable. It could have been a lot worse, even. A few hundred years past it had been built from state of the art solar nanocrete, and that was tough stuff, so it had held up to the years more than might be expected. A big chunk just north of the inn was still collecting solar, even. I had plugged into it some time back, figuring free power was free power. Running a cable had been easy enough. Connecting up at the end had been a bit more tricky, since nobody made the necessary plugs anymore, but I'd figured out a way to splice in eventually.

With a blink I saw something else come into sight around a clump of juniper trees that partially blocked my view of the road. It was a man. Just an ordinary-looking human, walking along the road near the edge, out of the way of what little traffic there was.

What the hell? It was well over four hundred klicks to Vegas. Had this guy walked all that way? He wasn't carrying so much as a backpack, and as he drew closer, I could see he was wearing perfectly ordinary boots. But there was only nothing and more nothing between the inn and the ancient city, so if he hadn't walked all that way, where had he come from?

Maybe somebody ditched him along the way, I thought, coming to the only possible solution to the puzzle that I could think of.

The stranger reached the point where the dusty gravel path to the inn forked off from the cracked black tarmac and turned in. I got a better look at him as he approached. He was wearing a nice one-piece shirt and dark slacks with a little trim down the side, the kind of thing that seemed to be in fashion right now. His boots were black and looked like they weren't particularly worn, so he definitely hadn't walked far.

He was tall, with broad shoulders, and he wasn't carrying any extra fat. And good god but he was too handsome to be true. His face was the definition of "chiseled", his slightly tousled auburn hair looking like he'd just come from a modeling gig, with just a hint of rugged stubble on his chin. His eyes were a clear, bright blue, and his skin was tanned but not at all weathered.

Hot damn, I thought. *If he's gay and single I'll count myself the luckiest man on the planet.* "Howdy," I called out as the stranger drew closer. "Welcome to the Only Chance Inn. Only thing there is before you get to Eslesee."

"Hello." The stranger smiled and gave a wave. "It's been a long day, so I'm glad this place is here."

"I'll bet. How far you been walking?"

The man smiled, showing even white teeth that were as perfect as the rest of him. "Far enough to have a fair appetite."

"Well, you're in luck, the restaurant's just about to open for dinner."

Now that he was close enough, the stranger stuck out a hand. "I'm Adam."

"Gerild. Good to meet you." I took his hand. His grip was firm, his skin smooth and cool. "I'll show you in to the restaurant." Normally I'd just direct a guest inside and let the bots take care of things, I was pretty hands-off in managing the inn, but the ever-so-handsome and ever-so-mysterious Adam made me want to stick close.

I led the way back through the lobby and into the restaurant, and saw Adam seated and given a menu.

"Paper menus?" said Adam, holding the flimsy sheet in his hand with an odd expression.

"We get some odd folks in here, not everybody has compatible readers for an e-copy."

"I see. Been a while since I saw one."

"Well, I'll leave you to look it over. Wave me down when you're ready to order."

Adam looked up, with a little twinkle in his eye. "No wait-bot either? You really are old-fashioned here."

"Ah, uh, there is a wait-bot if you'd rather." I felt myself flushing. "I just haven't got squat to do right now, so I might as well keep busy." *And you're right easy on the eyes*, I didn't say.

"Fair enough." Adam flashed another perfect smile, then turned his eyes to the menu, and I retreated.

When I returned to take Adam's order I got one more of those smiles, and a little touch on the arm as Adam thanked me. The contact sent a pleasant tingle down my spine. It had seemed deliberate. *This might just be my lucky day.*

By the time I started clearing away the dishes from the small mountain of food Adam had ordered I was sure it was. The incredibly handsome man had flirted with me every time I came by. I did my best to flirt back. I'd never been very good at flirting, but I hoped I'd gotten my interest across. Another pair of customers had arrived in the meanwhile, but I let the wait-bot get them.

When they'd settled up, Adam said, "You have rooms for the night, I assume?"

"Yup." Deciding to go ahead and make a move, I said, "I've got two kinds. Basic room's sixty a night, comes with one bed. Or there's my room. Which is free. And also comes with one bed."

Adam blinked at me for an instant, then broke into a broad grin. "I see! Well, I do try to be frugal. I think your room sounds like just the thing."

I couldn't help but grin back. The little tingle that had been running down my spine turned into an anticipatory warmth located somewhere a little further south. If that kept up my jeans were going to be getting a bit tight, but Adam was already climbing to his feet, so he was apparently in no mood to wait. "I'll show you up," I said.

"Lead on."

My room was bigger than the others at the inn, as I had my desk and com gear set up in a little office at one end, but it was otherwise much the same, just a simple space with a bed, side table, and a few comfortable chairs. A big window looked out towards the road, but the curtains were drawn over it, hiding the light of the setting sun.

Adam surveyed the room and gave a little nod. "Nice place."

"Thanks." I caught myself scuffing a boot against the carpet like a nervous kid and stopped. "So, uh…"

Adam took a step closer, standing close enough to make it obvious he was a few inches taller. I tipped my head up, feeling that heat grow stronger and my jeans grow tighter. God, but I wanted Adam. Adam smiled another perfect smile, taking one more step, and tipped his head down to kiss me. Not a soft kiss or a sweet one, but a hot, hard, passionate kiss. His arms went around me, and I responded in kind, pulling the handsome stranger in tight.

When we broke off, I found myself breathing faster. "You sure don't waste any time," I said.

Adam chuckled. "Should I?"

"Hah. Nope." I pulled my hat off and tossed it at a chair, then started undoing buttons on my shirt. We both undressed with speed, neither of us apparently wanting to wait at all. Adam, without so many buttons to worry about, was nude first, and I paused for a moment to take in the view. Adam's body was just as chiseled as his cheekbones. He looked like he'd just stepped out of some kind of advertisement. He was just too damn good to be true. I was in decent shape myself, since I worked pretty hard to keep things up here, but there was no way I could be as perfectly sculpted as he was.

He was big too, his cock easily one of the largest ones I'd seen in real life, though nowhere near as giant as the weird, amped-up, unreal stuff you see sometimes in porn.

Realizing I was staring, I flushed and quickly finished stripping off my own clothes. Adam had climbed into the bed, and I got in with him willingly. I had the sudden thought, as we pressed together in another kiss, skin to skin, that I was very glad I was up to date on my prev shots. I'd hate to have to call this off, or hunt down a condom and hope I had some that hadn't expired.

Adam's kiss grew more and more heated, his tongue pushing into my mouth to twist and battle with mine. His hands started wandering, touching all over. His fingers were strong as they groped and kneaded at me, and I couldn't help but feel a further thrill. My cock was already erect, but my pulse raced even faster. I liked a guy who took charge, and Adam was pushing all those buttons, hard. He pushed them harder still when he suddenly rolled me over, pinning me down, and ground his hips against me. I groaned, putting my hands on Adam's backside and pulling him in close, feeling Adam's hot cock rubbing against my own.

Adam leaned back, looking down at me with a smile. "Like that?"

"Oh yeah."

"You might like this then." Suddenly he'd grabbed my wrists in an iron-hard grip and was bucking his hips, rubbing his cock against mine again as he held me down. My breath drew in sharply in shock, my body arching under Adam as pleasure and excitement both shot through me. Adam chuckled. "Thought so. You got some lube? If you like it rough, I'd probably better use some."

Feeling flushed but not quite able to be embarrassed, I nodded.

Adam climbed off of me, and I rose and fetched the bottle. Adam plucked it from my hand and set it on the nightstand. "There. But first..." He pulled me into the bed, kissing me again, then reached down, his fingers curling around my cock.

"Ah, god." Adam's strong hand gripped me firmly, starting to stroke, sliding my foreskin back and forth. I felt nearly half way there already. Adam's aggressive approach was turning me on massively. Adam bent his head, then, taking my cock into his mouth. I gasped, a shudder going through me. I threw my head back on the pillow, and my hands went to the back of Adam's head. "God," I moaned again.

Adam hummed softly around my cock—a sound of almost smug satisfaction—and intensified his work there, sucking and lapping at it hungrily. I moaned helplessly, feeling my pleasure building. I wasn't sure I'd come this fast since I'd been a teen, but Adam was getting me so incredibly wound up that I couldn't hold back.

A moment later I was there, building heat suddenly flashing to white-hot ecstasy as my cock pulsed in Adam's mouth. Adam didn't pull back, if anything he sank down deeper, swallowing every drop that shot out into his mouth.

When I was spent, Adam sat back with one more swallow and grinned. "Well, that was a lovely appetizer. Now, about the main course…" He grabbed the bottle of lube and pulled the top off. "Why don't you roll over and let me put this where it'll do the most good."

I didn't reply, I just rolled onto my stomach, spreading my legs apart.

A moment later I felt Adam's fingers probing at me, slicked with the lube. They pushed in, spreading it on me and stretching me out. Adam took a little more time here, making sure I was thoroughly relaxed and ready before finally withdrawing his fingers. I looked back over my shoulder and saw Adam spreading lube on that massive cock, before setting the bottle aside and moving to straddle me. His cock pressed at my backside, and I let out a soft moan, trying to stay relaxed. Adam pushed forward, slowly sinking into me, filling me up. His cock was enough to stretch me to the point of pain, but I managed to take all of it, though I was pretty sure I'd have been in trouble if he'd been even a millimeter larger in any direction.

"Mmm. You are nice and tight," said Adam in my ear as he rested above me.

I couldn't think of anything at all to say, but I apparently didn't need to, for Adam almost immediately began thrusting, letting out a low grunt of pleasure as he moved in a steady rhythm. Each long stroke sank deep, Adam grinding his hips down on me every time. With his huge cock stretching me out and pushing far into my depths it was an intense experience. I could feel my own cock becoming hard again beneath me.

It grew even more intense as Adam began thrusting faster. He was panting now, his breath harsh in my ear as he bent over me. I moaned, the mingled pain and pleasure as Adam took me hard and fast thrilling through me. I clenched down on Adam's cock as it invaded me over and over, my moans growing louder as Adam's thrusts grew harder still.

"Ah fuck, yes," groaned Adam, the powerful thrusts now irregular, jerky, but losing none of their strength, slamming into me hard and deep. Then with a loud grunt and a profound shudder Adam came, hot seed pumping out into me, Adam's pulsing cock filling me with a flood of thick cum.

I shuddered too, pleasure racing through me. I always loved it when my partner came, in some ways it was the best part of sex.

The moment eventually passed and we lay still for a time. My breath gradually slowed, and I felt Adam atop me likewise relaxing. Adam's cock within me relaxed as well, slipping from me. With a long sigh he rose. I sighed too, half in regret, half in appreciation of the way I could now take a full breath without the other man's weight atop me. As wonderful as that had been, practical reality always intruded far too soon.

"Thank you," said Adam, his voice soft, less assured than it had been. "I needed that."

"Been a while?" said I with a small smile. It had been a while for me as well, though not as long as some dry spells I'd had.

"Not exactly. It's just that sometimes…" He hesitated, and gave a little shake of his head. "Sometimes I need to feel like I'm human."

•   •   •

I leaned my head against Rolly's shoulder, taking in the moment. It was just past dawn, and I'd already been working for about an hour. Saddling up the horses counted as work too, of course, but that didn't mean I couldn't take some time to relax while I was doing it. The tall stallion didn't seem to mind as I leaned on him, he only whickered softly.

The warm smoothness of his hide was comforting. As much as having a truck or a car of some kind might sometimes be easier, I really liked having horses. I only had two at the moment, though once Star in the next stall over came into season, I hoped to get another.

"Morning."

I looked up to see Adam standing in the stable. "Hey there."

"That's a pretty nice horse."

"You know horses?"

He shrugged. "Only a little. But he's very striking."

I smiled. Rolly was a blood bay, which meant his coat was a deep chestnut that was nearly red, and his mane and tail were jet black. He also had black "socks" on his feet, which was a fairly dramatic coloring. Star was a lighter chestnut, just one color all over save for the small white star on her forehead. Not as showy, but I figured she and Rolly could make some very pretty babies if I was lucky.

I put the bridle over Rolly, getting him ready to put in his own day's work.

"Mind if I hang around, or should I leave you to work?"

"Nah, you can stay," I said. Having company was nice sometimes. I could get sick of it eventually, but other than the bots I was often alone here, so for now I was happy to have Adam around. "Though we'll be heading out in just a bit."

He nodded and leaned against the stable wall. "You been running this place long?"

"My whole life, it feels like," I said. "But nah, about ten years. It was my great-uncle's before that. I used to visit as a kid, and when I was about sixteen I started helping run things. He wasn't in great shape, had about ten different kinds of cancer for a few years there, so he needed a hand. I guess that was enough for him to leave the place to me."

"You like it here?"

"Yeah. It suits me." I heaved the saddle over Rolly's back, and bent to do up the girth strap. Rolly was pretty decent-tempered for a stallion, so he stayed put while I got it snugged down around his barrel.

"What about you? You got a steady job, home, wife and kids, that kinda thing?" I flashed him a smile, to let him know I wasn't being too serious.

He chuckled. "Not remotely. I'm pretty much just going from nowhere to nowhere. I don't need much to get by, so I haven't had a steady job in ages."

I nodded, though he looked way too neat and fashionable to be the kind of wanderer he seemed to be describing. I wondered suddenly if he was actually hooking his way around. Certainly he'd gotten out of spending anything on his room here with sex. He could probably get pretty far that way, given his looks. I sure wouldn't mind having him around longer if he wanted to stay. On which subject... "Hey, you know how to ride?"

He blinked at me. "I'm a little rusty, but I've been on a horse before."

"Want to come ride the lines and check things with me? Star there's pretty mellow, she's an easy mount for somebody not real experienced."

He hesitated a moment, then said, "Sure, why not?"

"I'll get her saddled up, then." Rolly tossed his head, obviously impatient with this delay, but I looped his reins over a peg in his stall and left it, going to get Star's bridle and saddle on. Adam stayed back and let me do the hard part. That was for the best, having somebody who didn't know what they were doing buckle on your saddle is a good way to fall off the horse sideways later on.

Adam swung up into the saddle if not with practiced ease, at least without any awkwardness. He sat on the horse with a decent natural posture too, though it was obvious he didn't really know what to do with the reins. That was fine; so long as he didn't do anything really stupid, Star would happily follow Rolly, she was used to that.

I mounted up too, and then spent a couple of minutes making sure Adam knew what to do with the reins and how to stop and start. I wasn't too worried, but it seemed to me like he'd enjoy the trip more if he didn't have to be a lump in the saddle. Then we set out into a clear summer morning, the sun already hot overhead, though it was nowhere near as scorching as it would get later.

We were riding through a juniper "forest" that covered the hills all around the inn. The tallest of the trees was barely ten meters, so they didn't exactly tower, and most were much shorter than that. They weren't clustered together either, each stood at least a few meters apart from its neighbors, but it was the closest thing to forest you could find around here, until you got well up into the mountains to the east.

The ground between the trees was red, and bone dry, dotted with scrubby sagebrush and the occasional prickly pear. The horses kicked up ruddy dust as they went, but the air was still and it settled quickly. It was a stark sort of landscape, but I liked it.

I'd been to a few other parts of the world when I was younger, but the desert would always be home.

Adam was pretty quiet as we rode, and I didn't say much either. We went along the cable that was pulling power from the road first, checking that nothing had fallen on it, that nothing had been chewing on it, and so on. I thought sometimes about burying it, but it was nearly half a mile long and that was a lot of trench to dig. None of the bots were really set up for digging, so I'd have to do it myself.

It meant I had to do these rides pretty regular, and that sometimes I had to patch the cable, but I didn't much mind, to be honest. I liked being out here with my thoughts. I glanced over at Adam. He was taking in everything around him, and a faint smile hovered at the corners of his mouth. It seemed he liked being out here too.

We went all the way out to where the cable plugged into the working section of the road. There weren't any problems, so we rode back at a faster pace. Adam still sat his saddle just fine while trotting, which took a bit more doing. He was all around too damn good to be true, and I found my mind drifting back to last night, to the fantastic sex we'd had. I hoped he'd stick around another night or two at least.

When we neared the inn I turned Rolly to go along the water pipe, which was partially buried, but mostly above ground. It climbed up into the hills behind the inn, until we got to the big cistern that fed it. That was buried at the crest of a hill, and I swung down from the saddle to haul open the top and check the water level. A smaller pipe fed into it, that ran up the hill from a spring below, and there was a little pump down there, with a solar panel to run it. It sent a constant, steady trickle into the cistern, and then as much water as we needed could be pulled from the big tank to flow down on pure gravity to the inn. Even if the pump failed, everything would be fine for days, so I'd have plenty of time to make repairs, so long as the level in the cistern stayed high.

The water was just to the leveling mark, so I shut it up again, and then we rode along the smaller pipe down to the spring, where the water I wasn't using made a little stream that ran along its course out into the desert. It dried up eventually, never making it to the nearest river.

The solar panel was clear and the pump was working away, so I turned the horse back around and we headed back the way we'd come. We rode in silence all that way, but as we crested the hill again, Adam said, "I always did like this part of the world. Places like this are apart, somehow. They don't change."

I nodded. "Yeah. You get out of sight of the road here, and you could be transported back a hundred, or a thousand years, and you'd never notice the difference."

"Exactly." Adam nodded. "Last time I was through here the road was different, and I don't think the inn was even there, but this," he gestured at the juniper forest around them, "was exactly the same."

I couldn't help but raise my eyebrows at that. The inn had been here for an awfully long time, and I couldn't even name the last time the road had gotten some kind of major change to it. Before I'd been born, that was for certain. I gave Adam a look, and found he was looking down at the saddle and not at me, his cheeks flushed. "You have some prolong treatments or something? You look awfully young to remember before the inn was here."

Adam cleared his throat and shifted in the saddle. "Yeah. Sorry, I don't like to talk about it."

"It's fine. I won't pry." I mentally filed away the fact that he was old, probably old enough to be my grandfather, but I wasn't sure what difference that made. He was a fascinating enigma, but none of it was any of my business unless he wanted it to be. So we finished out the ride in silence, which still felt pretty comfortable, and I unsaddled the horses and brushed them down, though the ride had been easy enough they didn't really need it.

Adam lent a hand with that, and he was a quick study, he only needed to be shown what to do once.

"Now that's all done, there'll be this evening's customers to deal with soon, and I don't want to smell like horse, so I'm heading up to have a shower." I shot Adam a smile. "You're welcome to come join me if you like."

"Sounds good to me," he said, and we went up to my room together.

I'd put in a very nice shower, a big tiled cube with the best low pressure shower head I'd been able to find. There was no tub, since I never took baths so it hadn't seemed worth bothering with. There was plenty of room for two, though, and Adam shed his clothes without hesitation and joined me under the hot spray. Next thing I knew he had me pinned up against the wall and was kissing me hard. I kissed back, the pleasant anticipation I'd been feeling instantly growing to a heated arousal. My cock, pinned between our bodies, grew swiftly erect, and I felt Adam's cock prodding at me too, a wonderfully hot hardness.

When he let me up from the kiss I scooted sideways and turned off the shower. "Can't waste water," I said, and then I kissed him again. He grabbed my wrists, pinning them to the cold tiles, and ground his hips against me. I moaned into the kiss. God, but I loved how aggressive he was about sex. It was just the best damn thing. His cock was rubbing against mine, and when he let go of my wrists it was to grab my own cock and pump it, making me moan again as he gripped it firmly.

He chuckled, obviously enjoying himself, and his other hand squeezed my balls, then pushed under them to run along my taint and press between my cheeks. "Shall I go get the lube?" he said.

My "yes" was probably a little too eager, and certainly a little breathless, but he only chuckled and ducked out of the shower.

He must have just about run across the room because he was back in only seconds, bottle in hand. He got a puddle of the stuff and plopped the bottle in the shower caddy, then pushed me up against the tiled wall once more. I didn't put up any resistance, I just put my arms around him as he worked his slicked fingers into me, pulling up my leg with the other hand so that he could get better access.

He took some time, stretching and preparing me, and I did my best to relax, letting my muscles come unclenched, hoping I'd be ready to take that massive cock again.

I expected him to turn me around, and was looking forward to being pinned to the wall and fucked from behind, that was the kind of thing I liked a lot, but next thing I knew he'd picked me up, my back still against the cold tiles but both feet off the ground, and just like that he positioned me and thrust in. I cried out with pleasure and pain both, startled and more turned on than I could have expected. All those trim muscles weren't just for show, he was strong as *hell*. He'd lifted me like it was nothing, and I was slim enough, but I wasn't exactly tiny.

Adam seemed to have no trouble at all keeping me held up, either, my knees to my chest, and his cock sunk deep in me. That felt absolutely amazing, and the thrill of knowing just how strong he was, just how close to helpless I was, was intense. It got even more intense when he started thrusting, driving his cock into me deeply, pushing me up against the wall with every stroke. I gripped his shoulders, my fingers digging in, and cried out repeatedly.

Then he kissed me, silencing me, his tongue thrusting into my mouth even as his cock continued to thrust into my ass. It was a relentless pounding, rough and fast, with no care for anything but his own pleasure, taking me hard. It was absolutely amazing, and I clenched down tight on his cock, my fingers digging hard into his shoulders as he just about pushed me through the wall with the force of his thrusts.

He broke off the kiss, panting, and with a few more short, rough thrusts he came, a flood of slick heat filling me, making me moan with it. He rocked his hips a few more times as his cock pulsed in me, then pulled out with a deep sigh and carefully let me stand on my own feet again.

I still clung to him, feeling more than a little weak in the knees. He kissed me again, hard and hot, and his hand wrapped around my cock, stroking it firmly. I moaned helplessly into the kiss, feeling completely overwhelmed by him, and in just seconds I came hard, my own seed gushing out over his hand.

He broke off the kiss and let go of me, giving me a satisfied, almost smug smile. I wobbled, then slid down the wall to sit on the shower's tiled floor, my legs too shaky to hold me up. "Fuck."

"I hope that's not a complaint?"

"Hell no! That was amazing."

"Oh good." With a chuckle Adam reached out and turned the water back on. He started washing the mess off of him, and after a while I managed to get back to my feet and do the same. We got ourselves washed, dried off, and dressed again in short order, and then it was time to go on with my day.

I treated Adam to lunch down in the diner, which had almost a dozen other customers. People sometimes came in waves like that, nobody for days and then we'd be full to the gills all at once.

Adam kept himself amused as I took care of business, but even when he wasn't there I kept thinking about him. The lingering soreness of my backside would have been a regular reminder even if nothing else had brought him to mind. He hadn't exactly been careful this time. I might need to add some padding to my saddle before riding the lines tomorrow.

Not that I was going to complain. A little soreness was a very pleasant reminder of what he'd done to me. As far as I was concerned he could pound me raw every day of the week and I wouldn't complain, it had been that good. I found myself hoping he'd stick around for a while. It wasn't just for the sex, either. I'd liked his company this morning. He was interesting, handsome and sexy as hell, and he knew how to let a silence sit without needing to fill it, which was a rare thing indeed. He seemed like a rare sort of man, and I'd be pleased if I could get to know him better.

•   •   •

Adam was still there come dinner time, though I let the wait-bot get him, since it was still hopping and I was busy getting people checked in.

I managed to swing by to drop off the check, though. I'd given him a hefty discount, I figured he was more than paying his own way, given how much I'd enjoyed him so far. "How was dinner?"

"Fine, just fine." He smiled up at me, still as absurdly handsome as ever. "So is that room special still available tonight?"

I grinned. "More so than ever, we're just about full. I'll be a while coming up, but you can go get the bed warmed up if you like."

"Sounds good to me," said Adam, and he touched my hand again, lightly. Somehow that was still electric, even after all we'd done. I felt my heart skip a beat, and I'll admit I shamelessly rushed through the rest of what I had to do to make sure all the guests were taken care of before just about running up the stairs to my room.

He was sitting sprawled in a chair when I arrived, his shoes and his shirt off, showing that fantastically muscled chest, but his pants still on. "Evening," he said, as I stepped in.

"Evening." I shed my own boots and hat right away, and took off my belt too.

"All done with your work?"

"Unless some emergency comes up, yep."

"Seems like you work hard here."

"Only sometimes. The bots do most of the real work. But I like to keep busy, just so I don't get bored." I grinned at him. "Though with you around there's a lot less danger of that."

He laughed at that. "I suppose that's good." Then he rose from the chair, and next thing I knew he'd wrapped his arms around me and was kissing me hard. I kissed back, pressing willingly into his embrace. He let go eventually, though, and said, "You up for another round tonight?"

I almost said yes instantly, but then I considered the sore state of my backside and reconsidered. I'd be unable to sit the saddle at all if we had another round like that last one. "Uh... Maybe if you go easy on me. I'm pretty damn sore still."

Adam chuckled. "There's other options. You like giving head?"

I felt a grin spreading on my face as I replied, "Oh yeah."

He laughed, probably at my eager expression. Next thing I knew he had undone his pants and was pulling his cock out. It was already half hard, and I licked my lips in anticipation just looking at it. "Why don't you give me a demonstration, then?" he said.

I dropped to my knees in front of him willingly and curled my hand around his monster member, enjoying the feel of it as I started to stroke. I leaned in and licked at the tip, feeling it grow and harden further in my grip. I took the head into my mouth, still stroking at the base with my hand, and started to bob my head back and forth in time with my strokes.

"Ah... That's good," said Adam, breathlessly. I made a little humming sound of satisfaction and increased my attentions, working my tongue against him.

His hand came up, resting on the back of my head, and I felt my heart race faster at that. I was already in a submissive position, on my knees like this, and as he began to work his fingers through my hair, gripping it firmly, a further thrill went through me. He twisted his hand in my hair hard enough to hurt, and started to rock his hips, pushing deeper into my mouth as he held my head in place.

I let go my grip on his cock and just concentrated on not gagging as he worked his way deeper in with each thrust. Soon his massive member was sunk all the way down my throat, choking me completely. I swallowed around it, and another shudder went through me as his second hand joined the first, holding me down hard on his cock for a long moment.

Finally he let me up, and I pulled back and caught my breath, but it hardly took the renewed pressure of his hands to get me to go down again, I was eager to please him. I loved doing this for a guy. There was just something about it, about the feel of a cock filling my throat, that felt good. I was proud of my ability to deepthroat, too, though Adam's massive cock was testing that to the limit. Still, I *was* doing it, and as he began to breathe hard and to move faster, fucking my throat now, I felt a sense of satisfaction, that became something like triumph when he pulled my head hard down one more time and started to come.

I tasted the bitter-salt taste of his seed, but only just barely, his cock was so far down my throat that most of it never even touched my tongue. I swallowed it down, a shudder of pure pleasure going through me.

Finally the last drops of it were done and he pulled back. I sucked in a badly-needed breath and leaned back. Adam smiled down at me. "You're pretty good at that."

"Thanks." I grinned up at him, feeling almost smugly satisfied, still breathing hard.

"Shall I return the favor?" he said.

I gave a shrug and got up from my knees. "If you really want to. I'm feeling pretty good about the state of the world already, though. Sex doesn't have to be a tit for tat thing every time."

"True enough." He pulled me in and gave me a kiss, softer than the last one, though it still had some heat in it. "Thanks, though."

"You're more than welcome. I like having you around."

He gave me a kind of funny look at that, but finally he said, "I like being here," before giving me one more kiss. When he let me go I dropped down onto the bed and started to get undressed. He was already most of the way there, and it wasn't long before we were both under the covers. He wrapped his arms around me without a word, and I pressed happily into that embrace. The sex with him had been great so far, but this was nice too. I was getting awfully fond of him. It was hard to think when I'd last liked a guy this much, this fast.

•   •   •

I heaved the saddle over Rolly's back, on another fine, clear morning. Adam leaned against the stable wall behind me, watching. He'd been here for just over a week now, and I was still pretty damn pleased to have him here. We'd had great sex every single day and sometimes twice a day, and his company was more than pleasant the rest of the time too. He'd taken to riding out with me every morning, and he sometimes lent a hand with the rest of the day's work as well, so it wasn't like having him around was getting in the way of my work or anything like that.

I'd be pretty content if he stuck around more or less forever, truth be told. "Want me to saddle up Star for you again?" I asked as I finished up with Rolly.

"Sure."

"Maybe I should teach you how. If you're going to stick around long term—which I'd like pretty well—you should know how to saddle a horse."

Something in his face changed, his smile vanishing, his expression going very still, very flat. "You know what, don't bother saddling Star after all. I have to go do something. I'll...see you around." He walked briskly out of the stable, while I stood there flat-footed, staring after him. What the hell had just happened?

I went to the stable door, and somewhat to my surprise I saw Adam literally running away, already half way down the dirt road towards the road proper. He was going at a pretty good clip, too. I scowled. I wasn't going to drag him back or anything, but it didn't seem right to let him just run off like that without at least trying to find out what the *hell* was going on. I ducked back into the stable and swung up on Rolly's back, then nudged him out of the building and after Adam.

He was already out of sight by the time I got moving, no doubt on the road itself and probably still running. I kicked Rolly into a canter along the dirt road, then pulled him to a halt when we reached the cracked nanocrete. I spotted Adam to the north and he looked already halfway to Eslesee. He was a mighty fast runner. I kicked Rolly into a full gallop, glad that this patch of the road was in better shape than some so I didn't have to worry about him turning an ankle, and we took off after Adam.

It soon became clear that we weren't catching up as fast as we should have. Rolly was no racehorse, but horses were faster than humans, at least over short stretches. I started to wonder if Adam was enhanced in some way. Might explain why he looked so damn perfect, if he had some kind of extra cybernetics going on or something. He hadn't seemed like any of the cyborgs I'd met, usually you could tell, they don't tend to be subtle about it, but it was possible.

I tried to urge a little more speed out of Rolly. I could just see Adam looking back over his shoulder at us. Suddenly he halted, apparently giving up. I let Rolly drop back to a canter so as not to wind him, then eventually pulled him to a halt in front of Adam, who stood in the middle of the road with his arms crossed, giving me a look that was just about a glare.

I glared right back, looking down from Rolly's back. "What the hell do you think you're doing?"

"Leaving. I'm allowed to, I hope?"

"Of course you're allowed to!" I slid out of the saddle to look him in the eye at his own level. "But it's awfully rude to just run off without a word in explanation. Especially considering, you know..."

He lifted his eyebrows at that. "You know?"

"That we've been fucking each other's brains out all week! And enjoying each other's company outside of bed too, I thought. I thought we were getting close."

"I don't get close to people." Adam's eyebrows went down, and his voice was hard, almost angry.

"Why the hell not? You're a great guy, handsome, articulate, nice... You got some kind of secret you're hiding?"

Adam growled, "Yes, in fact, I do."

"Oh." That took some of the wind out of my sails. Still, I wasn't going to just back off and wave goodbye at this point. "I guess I can get not wanting to share something personal with a guy you've known only a week. But dammit, if you've got some deep dark reason you can't stay, I'd have liked knowing that up front, before I started getting attached, you know?"

"I'm sorry," he said, and he looked down at his feet. "I hadn't expected to stay past the first night. Just..."

I felt a little cheered at that. "So you do like me, then?"

That got a deep sigh out of him. "I shouldn't."

I couldn't help but ask, "Why not?"

He shot me an annoyed look. "You are awfully persistent."

"Well forgive me for wanting to know why one of the nicest guys I've ever met and best lays I've ever had is dumping me."

He gave me a long, silent look, and I got a sudden urge to fidget, but managed to not. I just looked back. Finally he heaved one more, deeper sigh, and said, "I'm not human."

I blinked at him, thinking that surely I'd heard that wrong somehow. "What?"

"I'm not human. That's why. I can't get close to humans because eventually I'll slip up, and they figure it out, and freak out on me. I'm not human."

"But... There's never been any evidence of little green men, nobody's ever broken the light speed barrier, and we'd spot anybody coming sublight from light years away. And nobody's ever managed to make true AI either. Humans are all there is. You *have* to be human."

He looked at me for a moment longer, then suddenly the color seemed to fade out of him. He went completely monochrome, a flat, faintly metallic gray, and then dissolved into a cloud of tiny particles, vanishing out into dust in seconds.

"Holy shit."

Dust recollected into a vaguely upright pillar, turned human-shaped, and took on color again, and he was standing exactly where he'd been standing a moment ago.

"Holy shit," I said again. "You're a gray man."

He heaved a sigh, shaking his head. "I never much liked 'gray men' for us. We're not a gray goo scenario, there never was any danger of *that*."

The gray man program had been meant to be humanity's next big leap forward, way back when. Somebody had come up with a way to make a swarm of microscopic machines work together seamlessly, forming a kind of robot colony organism that was capable of all kinds of amazing feats. Some industries still used the basic model as infinitely flexible robot workers.

Programmed correctly, though, the particles could join together like brain cells and imitate a human brain as well as it could imitate anything else. A human brain, scanned completely, could then be downloaded into it. The idea had been to copy the dying into such immortal, vastly capable, infinitely moldable bodies, and let them live forever. But the program hadn't gone at all as the designers had hoped. "I thought they were all killed, though? It was something almost like a war. I've seen old holo footage of it." Footage of ordinary meat-humans and their machines trying to somehow fight and kill rampaging clouds of silver that could be human one instant, living weapons the next, and a thousand scattered pieces, impossible to track and find, the moment after. It had been brutal and bloody and disturbing. I'd seen one especially bad holo of a seemingly ordinary human walking down a crowded city street, before shattering suddenly into self-propelled razors that had sliced innocent bystanders to bloody shreds, and I knew that was the least of what the gray men had done as humanity had hunted them down.

I looked at Adam, and I found my hand was resting against the grip of my bead pistol. I moved my hand as soon as I realized what I was doing, though. For one thing I could empty the whole magazine into him and it'd accomplish nothing. I might break a few microscopic nano-components, but the rest would just scatter, the way I'd seen happen in that old war footage, and when they came together again he could kill me easily.

More than that, though, I didn't *want* to shoot Adam.

His eyes rested on my hand, and I knew he'd seen the instinctive reaction. His expression was deeply sad. "The ones who went insane were killed," he said softly. "Which was over ninety-eight percent of us. There were three of us who stayed sane."

I drew in a sharp breath at the sheer awfulness of that. "So there's only three of you in the world?"

"In all the universe," he said. His mouth quirked slightly in a bitter smile. "One I can't stand, we've been avoiding each other for centuries. The other went off to one of the colonies by generation ship a few centuries ago. I think he hoped they might forget about the horrors of the war against us out there. Maybe they will, they actually wanted to have him, since he'd survive the whole voyage, so somebody consistent would be there all the way along."

"That's...awful lonely."

Adam's eyes were distant, seeing the past. "I'd rather be alone than be surrounded by people studying me like some kind of...thing. They kept us sane ones locked away for years, you know. Even after they let us out, the government tracked our every move. But that government doesn't exist anymore." His gaze came into focus, his eyes fixed on me suddenly. "So no human being knows I'm still alive. Except you."

I shook my head. "Wow. But... That's crazy. I mean, this was all the United States back then, wasn't it? That was, uh...a lot of years ago." I had not exactly been an avid student of history, and I'd certainly never been good at memorizing dates. The extermination of the gray men had been after the first hot war, I was pretty sure, and before the first interstellar colony ship, but I didn't know exactly when.

"A little over fifteen hundred years," said Adam, still soft, still sad.

"Wow." I looked at him. His expression was distant again; he wasn't meeting my eyes. "I imagine you've been pretty lonely through most of that."

"Yes."

"You've never...settled down, lived with somebody? I would think being alone for centuries would drive somebody mad just as much as having their brain re-written."

He met my gaze for a moment, then looked away again. "A few times. The last was about four hundred years ago. I probably don't have to tell you why I'm not still with him." His mouth set in a hard, bitter line.

"I'm sorry."

He didn't reply. I wasn't sure what to say either, and we both stood around for a moment, kinda awkwardly. I scuffed the ground with one boot and finally said, "I get why you want to go, and you can if you want. I won't keep you. Hell, I couldn't keep you if I tried! So you don't have to stay." I took another step closer to him then, and got close enough to reach out and take his hand. "But I wish you would."

He snatched his hand back from me. "Don't you get it, Gerild? I'm not human! At all!" Suddenly he flashed into another shape, something like a dragon, fanged and ferocious, right in my face. Then a kind of robot or android, then half a dozen totally different people in quick succession, followed by a tiger, what I think was a dinosaur, and a flock of birds that whirred around, then slammed into each other to melt into a blob of gray stuff, before going back to the shape I was used to seeing, just as handsome as ever. I'd flinched in surprise at the dragon, and I heard Rolly behind me snort and shy, but I managed to stand my ground through the rest of it. "Don't you understand?" Adam shouted once he was himself again, "I'm not even the same species as you! Homosexual means liking your own kind! I'm nothing like your kind! I'm not a man! I'm not human!"

I couldn't help it. I knew it was probably the wrong thing to do and I was going to piss him off, but I let out a snort of laughter.

"What's funny about any of this?" he snapped.

"I'm not homosexual. I'm bisexual," I said, trying not to laugh more.

He blinked at me, anger cut off by surprise. "What?"

"I'm also kinky as *hell*. You are pretty much saying you can be my every fantasy if you want to be. I get why you might not want to settle down and form attachments, but from my point of view you haven't said anything that ruins your appeal for me. Just the opposite, in fact. So you're not exactly scaring me off here."

"But... You said earlier that you've seen footage of the fighting, back when the others went insane..." His brows were furrowed, his expression puzzled.

"It was pretty grim watching, yeah. But if after fifteen hundred years you haven't lost the plot and started murdering everything in sight, I don't think you're going to start now. I'm not afraid of you. I meant it that you can go. I also meant it that you can stay. Really."

"I..." His blue eyes were troubled, and I could tell he was torn. I knew it must be hard for him. He was accepting future pain, one way or another, if he got closer to me. We couldn't have a "happily ever after" when his "ever after" was infinite compared to my regular old human life. Maybe it was selfish of me to even think of asking him to risk that kind of heartbreak.

All the same, part of me wanted to make crazy declarations of love and beg him to match them. I really did want him to stay. I'd meant every word of what I'd just said. I was pretty sure telling him I loved him would be a bit too much, though. Trying to keep things casual, trying to let him know that I wouldn't ask more than he wanted to give, I smiled and said, "I don't know if that free room deal is going to be open forever, mind. I can't keep freeloaders around. You should take advantage of it while you can."

His troubled expression wavered, one corner of his mouth quirking up in the smallest possible hint of a smile. "I never have managed to save up much money."

"You have to be frugal, then."

"Yeah."

"Well, sleeping along the road is free, it's very true. But my bed is free as well, and it's much more comfortable." I held out my hand to him, and he hesitated just a moment more, then took it.

His hand felt warm, indistinguishable from human, and I squeezed it gently, smiling at him.

"Thanks," he said.

"You're more than welcome." Rolly hadn't gone anywhere when he shied, thankfully, so I got ahold of his reins. I dropped Adam's hand and swung up into the saddle, then held my hand out again. Rolly could carry double easily enough. Adam took my hand again, and I managed to haul him up with his help. He settled on the saddle-pad behind me, sliding his arms around my waist. I freely admit I leaned back into that embrace just a little bit before settling into a proper seat and nudging Rolly forward.

We went at a walk now, there was no rush and I didn't want to dump Adam off. He might not take any harm from it, given what he was, but it would still be rude. Speaking of which... "Would it be rude of me to ask a few questions about how things work for you? I'm awfully curious."

I felt his shrug. "I don't mind. I'm not...used to talking about it much, but since you know already, I don't mind sharing the details."

"I have to admit, right now my mind's mostly just wondering what the hell I swallowed last time I gave you head."

He laughed at that. "Well, there wasn't any sperm in it, but it wasn't an, ah, actual piece of me, or anything like that. The...system I guess, the parts, makes imitations of things like spit and semen and even piss. I wouldn't pass well for human if I didn't have those things.

Although it can only happen if I drink enough water and eat enough organic stuff, but that doesn't really take much."

"Is that the reason why you eat food, then?"

"I need fuel, same as anybody, I'm just more efficient than a human would be. I could eat anything that can be broken down, so pretty much anything organic. I get feedback that's pretty much just like taste, though, so I do like eating food more than random objects. Food flavors are more interesting and complex than just eating grass or wood or whatever's handy."

"You said you're not a gray goo. So you can't eat rocks or metal, or things like that?"

"Heh. I can, but that's to gain mass, not for fuel. Different purposes."

I blinked. "You can be bigger?"

"If I want to be. Makes it hard to pass for human, though, and there are other limits."

"Wow." My mind was immediately supplying a bunch of pretty wild fantasies. I'd always had a bit of a kink for size difference. I'd liked how tall he already was pretty well, but the idea that he could be taller as well as differently shaped was fascinating. "So I take it you look like a men's fashion model because you want to?"

That got a chuckle. "Pretty much. My original body was, well... Failing. Old, sickly, ugly."

"Happens to most of us eventually." I gave a shrug. "You don't look at all like your old self?"

"My face is similar, a little bit. But it was too tempting to be the...best version of me, I guess. How could I not?"

"I'd do the same if I could," I admitted.

"You look good the way you are," he said, his voice a little softer, a little warmer, and he squeezed me around the waist.

I felt myself blushing. "If you say so," I replied.

He chuckled. "It's true. You have any more questions?"

"Uh... I'll probably have a million more eventually. Right now I can't think of many. Uh. Oh, I guess your clothes must be part of you too, since they dissolved with everything else?"

"Yep."

"So you were just taking off pieces of yourself when you stripped? That's a little weird."

He shrugged again. "I'm pretty used to it. I *can* wear ordinary clothes. But it's simpler to not have to worry about it."

"I bet. Means you have a basically infinite wardrobe."

"I'm not great at design. I just copy things I've seen."

I thought of another question, then. "You obviously feel, er, pleasure. Can you feel pain too?"

"I can, but I can turn it off if I want to. I can turn off the pleasure as well, I can more or less direct my senses however I like. I could taste with my whole skin, or feel no tactile feedback at all, if I wanted. Though it's easy to accidentally damage myself or others without tactile sense and without pain. Squeeze things too hard, walk into things I didn't notice, stuff like that. So mostly I feel pain and pleasure both more or less the way a human would."

"Is sex the same, then?"

"Nearly. Now that I'm used to the way things feel in this body in general. The programmers told me they did the best they could to make some things feel the same, when they designed the system. They knew there would be shocks when we were copied over, and hoped that having things like the ability to taste food, the ability to have sex, would help keep us sane. Obviously that didn't quite work out." He paused and then heaved a sigh. "It...helps, at least."

I remembered, suddenly, that first night, and him saying he needed to feel human. I leaned back into him some more. We were almost back to the inn by now. "I'm pretty glad you like it. Sex with you is some of the best sex I've had." I thought again about all the different shapes he'd taken. "And I have to admit I have...thoughts about what else we might do now."

He chuckled softly at that. "Yes, you did say you were kinky."

"As hell. But out here in the middle of nowhere I don't get a lot of chances to indulge. Mostly I watch porn. Usually that seems frustrating, since so much of what you see in it isn't physically possible, but, well... I'm kinda hoping..." A lot of my favorite genres were CGI-heavy things that got into weird realms of inhuman fantasy, so I had never dreamed I'd get to actually do anything from them.

He nuzzled against the back of my neck, sending a pleasant shiver through me. "I'll see what I can do."

We reached the inn then, and he slid down off of Rolly's back. I climbed off as well and gave him a look. "I, ah... I have to take care of Rolly, he needs a rubdown after that run, but I was thinking of just checking in that the bots have things under control and going up to my room after. If you, er...don't mind that."

He gave me a grin. "I don't think I mind at all. I'll go up and wait, and think of interesting things to do to you until you get there."

I felt my cheeks flush bright red at that, but I smiled as I led Rolly to the stable, a shiver of pleasant anticipation going down my spine. I wasn't going to be irresponsible enough to neglect the horse, but I think I gave him the fastest rubdown I'd ever managed before getting him put away in his stall. I swung by the front desk, where I found Jack plugged into the terminal there. He had things well in hand, so I just told him I'd be taking a few hours off and ran up to my room, taking the stairs two at a time.

I stepped into my room, and Adam was sprawled out on the bed, every inch of his body gloriously nude. I felt a bolt of pure lust go through me at the sight of him. I wanted some of those wild fantasies, but I'd take him just the way he was, too. He looked good.

"Hello there, cowboy," he said with a grin. "Why don't you come in, get a little more comfortable, and let me know just what sorts of things you had in mind when you talked about kinky fantasies."

"Yes, sir," I said, only half ironically, and grinned right back. I pulled my hat off and tossed it onto the chair, then started undoing shirt buttons. "So..." I cleared my throat, trying not to feel self-conscious, though I knew my cheeks were probably pretty red. "There's a lot of strange stuff out there. I don't know how much porn you watch..."

"Enough." His grin grew broader as he watched me blush. I shifted my weight around, but finished taking my shirt off.

"Well, after seeing you turn into all those creatures, I was, ah, thinking about feral. You know what that is?" In some ways "feral" porn was tame, as fetishes went. In other ways it was fairly wild, for it was all about sex with animals. But feral as a genre was distinct from bestiality, for in feral porn the animals were portrayed as intelligent, often even capable of speech. To me that had always mattered. I couldn't watch straight up animal porn, not even knowing it was all faked by computer, as most porn was, but something about the primal nature of feral porn, of being with something so utterly inhuman, yet still capable of thinking desire, was a massive turn on for me.

Adam really had no idea how much his being what he was seemed like a plus rather than a minus.

Though maybe by now he did, for his grin stayed put and he nodded. "Oh yes. Any specific, ah, species in mind?"

I shook my head. The details didn't matter that much, only the sense of being taken by something wild and primal.

Adam turned gray again, his form stretching and shifting, and when it took on color once more there was a tiger lounging in my bed. "How's this?" The grin was somehow still the same, despite the long fangs now involved, and it sent a shiver down my spine. I was already getting hard, and he hadn't even done anything yet.

I licked my lips as I looked him over. "That's...really good." Though I did notice one difference from the fantasy. He was actually a very small tiger. The real thing tended to weigh a fair bit more than a human did, so that made sense. "It's nearly perfect. Though, uhm, if it's not too much trouble…"

"Hmm?" He tilted his head to the side, ears swiveling as he gave me a curious look. God damn, there was a *tiger* in my bed! It was unreal and amazing, and I just about wanted to forget about my last request and jump on him. Or have him jump on me. But I'd brought it up, so I plowed ahead anyway.

"I like...size differences. You said you could be bigger if you need to?"

He gave me an amused look. "I can't rob Newton. To get bigger I need a source of mass. So unless there's something around the room that's decent sized that you don't mind me destroying, I can't be larger, no."

I glanced around. "Ah hell. The chair there's always been a little wobbly no matter what I do, and I've been meaning to replace it. So if you don't mind…"

"I don't. Though I'd prefer you didn't watch." He didn't blush, but there was a twist of discomfort in his voice. I gave a nod and turned towards the door, closing my eyes while I was at it.

There was a soft thud behind me as he jumped off the bed, and then there was near silence for a while; apparently whatever he did while "eating" in that way wasn't very loud. I could hear a faint kind of rustling, just on the edge of hearing, and that was it.

"You can look again," he said, and I turned around. He looked nearly twice the size he'd been, which was to say at least twice *my* size. The chair had been big, but not that big, and part of my mind was busy wondering if he'd done something with density, but the rest of me was fixated on other thoughts entirely. I felt a shiver of something like fear run down my spine. There was a massive predator right here in my room, more real than I'd ever thought possible, even if he wasn't "really" a tiger.

Next thing I knew he'd pounced on me, knocking me to the floor. I yelped, landing on my ass and sprawling backward, yelping again in shock as his teeth met just inches in front of my face.

Adam laughed, then licked his muzzle with a long, pink tongue, sitting back so that he was no longer pinning me. "I think you'd better get the rest of your clothes off right now," he said. "Unless you want me to ruin them, that is. Because they're coming off one way or another." He flexed his claws, curved ivory blades visible on each digit, and I felt another of those pleasantly fearful shivers. I started to swiftly shed my pants and underwear. I had gotten the pants off but had only just begun to pull my boxers down when Adam shoved me over further, his paws heavy, the leathery pads of them hot against my skin. I could feel the prick of claws, which sent my heart pounding, and it pounded even faster when he hooked his claws in the waistband of my boxers and yanked, shredding them even as he pulled them off.

He loomed over me, his breath a hot wash as he bent close, soft fur rubbing against my cheek in an animalistic nuzzle and then enormous fangs that could have torn my throat out nipping at my ear. I gasped and moaned, I couldn't help it. I was turned on like hell, my cock hard as a rock. I felt the brush of his fur against it as Adam crouched over me, pressing his body to mine. I felt something else too, a hot hardness that rubbed against my thighs as he continued to bite at my ear. His own cock was hard and ready too. An intense shiver of pure anticipation went through me at the feel of it, and I couldn't keep myself from reaching down to it, letting my fingers explore it.

It was massive, even bigger than Adam's cock had been before, and it was shaped differently as well, with a more pointed head and a swelling bulge at the base. I swallowed hard at the thought of that alien, animal thing going in me, another shudder of fearful, taboo delight going through me. I stroked my hand along the length of it repeatedly. He humped into my hand for a moment, the heavy balls hanging below his shaft bumping against me, then pulled back.

"Get up on the bed," he said, his voice a low growl.

I scrambled swiftly to obey. I had barely gotten onto the bed when he pounced again, his body shoving mine flat, his claws pricking as his paws pinned my shoulders down. I let out a startled cry, then moaned as he ground his hips against me, that huge, animal cock rubbing at my backside. He sniffed at me, then lapped the back of my neck. "You smell good," he said. "I want to just take you, rut you into the bed, even if it hurts you. You couldn't stop me if you wanted to."

"Ohgod." The breathless curse was completely involuntary. My cock was a throbbing ache beneath me and I nearly wanted to beg, to ask him to do just that. He chuckled in my ear, and then I heard a faint clink of a bottle, and next thing I knew something was pushing the slick wetness of lube between my cheeks, making me gasp in shock. His paws were still pinning me, and it wasn't his cock, it was something like a finger, but it was squirming and swelling in me and oh *god*, he'd made a tentacle or something to prepare me. I felt it twisting and pulsing, growing in me, stretching me out, and I whimpered as it began to stretch me further. I was panting hard, feeling almost overwhelmed by the strangeness of it, the reminder of just exactly how utterly inhuman Adam really was.

"Relax," he murmured in my ear, still crouched over me, paws on my shoulders. I drew in a deep breath and let it out, realizing how much I was clenching down on the thing wiggling in me. If I was going to take that massive tiger cock I was going to have to relax, he was right.

Slowly I managed to unclench my muscles, and slow my breathing. I closed my eyes, another shudder going through me as the whatever it was stretching me grew a little larger. It pulsed steadily, each pulse subsiding a little less than the previous, each one making it just that tiny fraction larger. It began to hurt, it was stretching me to the very limit, but it was amazing, and I moaned as it squirmed within me.

The tentacle withdrew, and I looked back over my shoulder, able to see that it had been the end of Adama's tail, formed into something that looked very like the cock I could also see peeking between his legs. He nipped the back of my neck, making me gasp again, and crouched lower, lining himself up, his furry body a heavy weight above me. The head of his immense cock pushed in easily, the pointed tip slender, but then the shaft began to stretch me out and I groaned.

Adam growled softly, nipping again, and started to rock his hips, working a little bit deeper with each stroke. I fought to stay relaxed. It was almost too much, and when the bulge at the base of it began to force me wider open still part of me almost wanted to tell him to stop. It hurt, even with the copious amounts of lube the tentacle had spread in me. But I wanted it. This massive creature was taking me, and it didn't matter that it hurt. The hurt was almost exciting, even, and when he bit my shoulder with a low growl and thrust forward, shoving himself in that last inch, the swollen bulge at the base of his cock popping inside me, I cried out with ecstasy as well as with pain.

For a long moment Adam just rested there, and I could hear him panting. Then he shifted, wrapping his forelegs around me, his chest pressing against my back, his fur soft and warm. He filled me more completely than I'd ever been filled, and my mind was already dazed with pleasure.

Then something began to squirm beneath my body as that alien tentacle wiggled under my hips and rubbed itself along my cock. I gasped, and Adam chuckled softly in my ear. The tentacle wormed its way to the head of my cock, and then to my shock I felt a warm slickness begin to enfold me, some kind of mouth opening up in it and slowly engulfing my cock. I moaned helplessly, a shudder going through me. Oh god, this was at least as bizarre, and at least as good as anything I'd ever seen in porn.

"You like that," murmured Adam.

"Yes," I panted. "God, yes."

He just chuckled again as his tentacle-mouth wiggled down to the base of my cock, ridges within it stroking over me, pulsing against me, hot and wet and wonderful.

Adam pulled his hips back slowly, his cock nearly as painful coming out of me as it had been going in, and then thrust in again, still slow, but firm, and I found my hands fisting in a double handful of blanket, a shuddering moan escaping me as I was painfully, wonderfully filled again. The tentacle still pulsed on my cock, ripples running along it, stroking up the length of me repeatedly, sucking at me hungrily.

He increased his pace gradually, but he wasn't exactly taking his time. I could hear his panting, feel his breath on the back of my neck as he bent over me, his paws clutching me, his cock thrusting into me, moving faster and harder with each thrust. The pulsing of the alien mouth around my own cock moved in time with it, sending waves of pleasure through me. I closed my eyes, writhing and moaning beneath him, totally caught up, completely overwhelmed. It was everything I'd ever fantasized about made real, and I could feel myself already on the edge, having to fight to keep from coming. I didn't want this to be over with too soon.

I couldn't help it, though. As Adam took me hard and fast, nipping at my neck and growling low in his throat, as his cock repeatedly filled me completely, as his alien tentacle stroked and caressed me, it was all too much and with a low groan of pure bliss I came hard, emptying myself into the sucking mouth around me, which seemed to simply drink down my seed. Was he absorbing it the way he'd absorbed the chair's matter? That thought sent another taboo thrill through me. I could never have pictured, only hours ago, that I'd be here, with a truly alien being, being taken so strangely, so improbably.

Adam paused his thrusting for a moment, staying sunk deep within me. The sucking mouth around my cock continued to pulse, milking the last drops from me.

With a rough nip he suddenly began to move again, pulling back almost all the way and slamming his full length into me with one brutal thrust, before settling into a hard, fast rhythm. "Ah!" I couldn't prevent my cry, and a second escaped me as he bit the back of my neck roughly. The tentacle-mouth still engulfed me, though its pulsing was slower, less insistent now. Adam, though, was moving ever faster, thrusting ever deeper, his breath fast and harsh as he took me with primal abandon. It was almost too much to take, pain nearly overcoming pleasure as he slammed his huge animal cock into me again and again.

Just when I thought I couldn't possibly take any more I felt the rhythm of his thrusts change, growing shorter, more jerky, and with a low grunt of pleasure he started to come hard, spurts of seed gushing out deep within me as he thrust in one last time.

My mind went nearly blank with the sheer pleasure of it. My every fantasy brought to life, this primal, animal rutting, filling me up with hot feline spunk, was wonderful beyond description, and I moaned as Adam emptied himself into me.

He let out a long, deep sigh and relaxed atop me for a moment. I grunted, half-crushed under the weight of him. Making fantasy real was not without its difficulties. Fortunately he seemed to recognize that he was too heavy, for after a moment he heaved himself up to all fours and got off of me.

I sighed as his cock withdrew from me, then winced as I shifted and felt the state of my backside. I was more than sore already, and I suspected I might have to skip tomorrow's line riding, because I wasn't going to be fit to sit down for some time, let alone get in a saddle.

Adam flopped over on his side on the bed, and then he went gray again, rippled, twisted, and a moment later he was himself, an ordinary if still ridiculously handsome man lying in my bed. I sat up slowly, and noticed a heap of gray powder on the floor behind him, the mass he'd shed in returning to his smaller shape, no doubt. I wondered what he would do with it.

"Did that live up to your expectations?" asked Adam. He was grinning still, but there was a hint of tension in his voice, and I knew the question was sincere.

Fortunately I didn't have to fudge the truth even a little. "And more," I said. "That was incredible." Then I remembered, suddenly, what he'd said about sex reminding him he was human, that first time. Did that mean he would like something like this less? "I hope you enjoyed yourself as well."

"Yes, very much so. It's good to play, to get to try out things without worrying about hiding who and what I am." His cocky grin softened to a more gentle smile. "I'm glad you've been so accepting of that."

"I can hardly complain, given what you just did to me. God. Though I'll regret it the next time I have to sit down." I gave him a smile of my own, and felt a certain warmth as I did that had nothing—or at least not much—to do with the sex. I decided I wanted to say something about that too. "I like you, you know. That doesn't mean you have to stick around any longer than you want to, I won't try to tie you down here. You're good company, though, putting all the sex and everything else aside too. I think you're the kind of guy I could spend a lot of time with. You can do whatever you want to with that, but I figured I should let you know."

Adam gave me a funny kind of look. "No 'I love you,' no 'together forever' or anything like that?"

"Nope." I shrugged. "Forever is ridiculous, since I'm only human. I know you're not, and I know promising you what I can't deliver would be doing you a cruelty, not a kindness."

"And you can't deliver love, either?" His look was level, serious.

I gave another shrug, feeling my cheeks flush. "I never said that. Just... 'I love you' isn't my style." It wasn't, though if I was being honest with myself, "love" might be at least close to the way I felt about him. He was the best thing that had ever happened to me, in more ways than one.

That got me a long, considering look from Adam. After a moment he smiled again. "I see. I suppose it's not my style either. But...I think that so long as the room stays free, I may be sticking around for a while."

I couldn't keep from smiling too as I replied, "Well, I'm not planning on raising the price."

   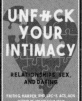